UNDERBELLY OF CAMBRIDGE

UNDERBELLY OF CAMBRIDGE

JOHN PHELPS

Matador
9 Priory Business Park,
Wistow Road, Kibworth Beauchamp,
Leicestershire. LE8 0RX
Tel: (+44) 116 279 2299
Fax: (+44) 116 279 2277
Email: books@troubador.co.uk
Web: www.troubador.co.uk/matador

ISBN 978 1788035 729

British Library Cataloguing in Publication Data.
A catalogue record for this book is available from the British Library.

Printed and bound in the UK by TJ International, Padstow, Cornwall
Typeset in 11pt Minion Pro by Troubador Publishing Ltd, Leicester, UK

Matador is an imprint of Troubador Publishing Ltd

CHAPTER 1

It happened at the worst possible time. It often did, though there never was a good time. What made it especially bad on this occasion was the fact that Frank had been free of his demons for almost a month and now they were back with a renewed intensity.

Bombs exploded inside his head. Disabled aircraft whined stridently before crashing to the ground, and there was the rat-tat-tat of machine gun fire. Even worse were the screams of women and children, as always the innocent, inevitable victims of conflict.

The sounds were soon supplemented by flashing images. There were sheets of flame, bayonets and boots sinking into pain-wracked bodies, torture chambers, faces contorted with hate, people falling into graves they had just dug, and soldiers with severed limbs or their insides hanging out. All were forcing their way into Frank's consciousness.

Worst of all was that unremitting, pitiless voice that said, "Kill! Kill! Kill!" over and over again.

Frank put his hands up to his ears in a vain attempt to block out the noises, pictures and, above all, that voice.

As usual, he began to retch. The beads of perspiration increased in size tenfold, the head throbbed, the pulse raced, the throat went dry. A full-scale panic attack was now imminent.

He had to get out.

Yet, just a few minutes earlier, he had been greeted warmly at the counter by an avuncular station sergeant and invited to take a seat while the man mountain he had helped to arrest was booked in and led to a cell.

The WPC whose aid he had come to had temporarily disappeared through a door at the side.

Then, perhaps because the sense of order in the small area near the counter was interrupted by the arrival of three more arrested drunks, those demons came storming back. They brought with them the sense of being boxed in, suffocated, potentially unable to move. Hyperventilation began to take hold.

"I've got to get out of here!" Frank said to no one in particular before fleeing to the street outside.

Once out in the open, he shot across the road, oblivious to honking horns, on to Parker's Piece. The famed Cambridge landmark was bounded on all four sides by busy streets. But at least it offered space… lots of it. Often a venue for fairs, cricket matches and other public events, the 'Piece' was at present offering something approaching tranquillity.

After a while, Frank stopped running and paused to do some breathing exercises, which he knew often helped in this sort of situation. He then did a dozen press-ups, followed by twenty star jumps. Eventually he was satisfied that the flashbacks had faded away and the voice, especially the voice, had been silenced.

He found a bench to sit on and spent some time gazing across the expanse of grass that was criss-crossed by concrete paths. As his composure began to return, he was able to observe a cricket pavilion and a hotel on the periphery and, across one of the roads away from the police station, a glass structure that housed a swimming pool. On Parker's Piece itself were pedestrians and cyclists on the paths, a few foreign language students picnicking and, in the distance, a group of young men kicking a football around.

Frank began to wonder what the police officers had made of his sudden exit. As he did, a young woman's voice could be heard suddenly a few feet away.

"Are you all right?" the woman asked. It was the young WPC whose aid he had come to a while ago. "Can I join you?"

"Yes, of course."

"I wanted to thank you for the way you helped me today, and then, when I heard you had left the station in a hurry, I began to worry about you."

"Oh, that's all right. My pleasure," Frank mumbled. He had come to the WPC's rescue outside a pub when he saw her being spat on, sworn at, manhandled and punched by an unruly man who was twice her size.

"I have to say you really impressed me with the way you handled that fellow," the WPC said. "His name is Rick O'Reilly and he's the most notorious bar room brawler in town. He's been in trouble no end of times, and he had just started yet another brawl in another pub.

Everyone was terrified of him and no one else thought to help when I was confronted with the situation whilst in that vicinity."

Frank felt no need to tell her that tackling one unarmed man, even one built like a colossus, was merely routine for him. His training, combined with natural strength and agility, had enabled him to cope with numerous, seemingly impossible situations.

On this occasion, Frank had told O'Reilly to leave the lady alone. O'Reilly had lunged at him and been disabled by a single, well-directed blow to the solar plexus. The subsequent short trip to the police station in a car that followed a Black Maria had, in fact, been far more gruelling as far as he was concerned.

"Glad to help," he said tersely.

"Well, thank you again. I am WPC Stephanie Shawcross and I should be obliged if you would provide us with a statement and perhaps act as a witness, assuming the case goes to court."

"No problem. I'm Frank Pugsley. I've just moved to Cambridge from Bristol. Please call me Frank."

Frank told WPC Shawcross briefly about his military background, which had included action in Iraq and Afghanistan.

"Unfortunately I still get flashbacks from time to time as a result of some of the things I experienced," he said, trying to sound casual.

The WPC nodded, and Frank sensed she was genuinely sympathetic.

"I'm afraid I'm none too clever when in confined spaces," Frank added. "I am now a civilian, unemployed and in Cambridge hoping to start a new life – though there's unfinished business to attend to first."

"I hope the new life compares favourably with the old," the WPC said.

Stephanie Shawcross was in her early twenties and only recently fledged in the police force. But her mind was sharp and her powers of observation acute.

She had no real knowledge of post-traumatic stress disorder (PTSD), but was aware of its existence and knew that military personnel who had experienced unimaginable wartime horrors were among the sufferers.

Frank Pugsley was in his early forties and, although only slightly above average height and of medium build, was immensely strong and athletic, she decided. His bearing was unmistakably military, and Stephanie was convinced that the suffering he had endured had had a profound influence on whatever human relationships he had been involved in. His hair was light brown and beginning to thin on top. His eyes were blue and piercing, and his face lean, slightly sallow and with more than a fair share of worry lines that lent themselves to a haunted look. She wondered how high a rank he had reached in the armed services and guessed that, despite the Bristol burr, he had been a major or a captain rather than a sergeant. The question intrigued her

Frank, meanwhile, began to make an assessment of Stephanie. Her hair was buttercup blonde, her cheeks rurally rosy and, although only 5ft 5in tall, she was sturdily built. He detected a Devon accent, a formidable intellect and whether he liked it or not an interest in him that went beyond professional.

"What sort of unfinished business were you referring to, if you don't mind my asking?" Stephanie could not resist putting the question to Frank.

Frank paused for a moment before replying: "I suppose there's no harm in you knowing. It's to do with the death of my son, Terry. He was just fifteen, and he had been hooked on heroin."

Stephanie could see the worry lines deepen and the blue eyes mist over.

"I had not seen him for nearly three years," Frank continued. "Perhaps things would have been different if I had been there for him."

"I'm so sorry," said Stephanie. "Please don't say anything else if you don't feel like it."

"That's all right," said Frank. "It helps to talk sometimes."

"Are you sure?"

"Yes, yes. I am in Cambridge to find out how he died. I want to catch up with the dealer who supplied him with those drugs, and I want to find out more about the circumstances surrounding his death. There are a lot of unanswered questions."

CHAPTER 2

Finding somewhere to spend the night was Frank's most pressing problem. He was new to Cambridge and would have preferred to have had more time to find the right spot to pitch his tent.

But the drama surrounding the arrest of O'Reilly, the fear of a major panic attack at the police station and his meeting with Stephanie Shawcross had made deep inroads into that time, and twilight was now imminent.

Frank found himself outside the Fort St George, a prestigious and imposing pub and eating place he had heard his wife talk about as somewhere popular to wine, dine and gaze across Midsummer Common on one side and the River Cam on the other. He quickly realised that, while the common offered space in abundance, it would be frequented by far too many revellers to make it a suitable place for sleeping.

So he began to cycle along the side of the Cam towards the city's periphery.

Before long, he passed under the Elizabeth Way road bridge and along the aptly named Riverside. Terraced houses looked out on to the narrow street, which was separated from the Cam by railings. A number of boats were moored to the side, and Frank guessed that at least some of them served as homes.

At the end of Riverside, kissing gates led to Stourbridge Common and, further along, a footbridge. It was now beginning to get dark and, although no spot seemed ideal, Frank decided to camp almost exactly in the middle of the common on the grounds that it was away from paths, banks and bridges.

The tent, which formed part of a backpack, was pitched in a trice. A couple of moments later, Frank was lying on his fold-up bed. But sleep eluded him. Frank was well used to camping out, or just sleeping under the stars for that matter. And he was always able to wake, rise and galvanise himself into action if the occasion demanded.

Groups of revellers, who were all merry rather than disorderly, could be heard wending their way home along the riverside path. A radio blared from one of the boats, a dog barked during its pre-bedtime walk, and the presence of cattle grazing on the other side of the river became apparent. None of these peace-time noises would generally be considered intrusive for a veteran of conflicts of all kinds like Frank.

Perhaps it was the fear that another PTSD attack would be triggered. Perhaps it was the day's dramas and the encounter with Stephanie Shawcross that refused to leave his mind. Perhaps, and even more likely, it was the question of what the next day had in store for him that kept him awake.

He was due to meet his estranged wife Laura and her new husband.

Frank sat up and did a bit of deep breathing. Then he fished out his Solitaire set and played until he was bored, and, eventually, he drifted into an uneasy sleep.

Dawn was heralded by voices from the footpath and from some of the boats, along with geese from the river, a rooster from what looked like a smallholding on the other side, the lowing of cattle, the barking of dogs and the calls and choruses of various wild birds.

The people with jobs to go to were on the move. Frank, whose orphanage upbringing preceded his military service, found he had more in common with people who had become known as Britain's underclass. Nine-to-five jobs, mortgages, rents, council tax and utility bills all seemed to belong to a world that had passed him by. These would be largely alien to the down-and-outs, too, though Frank was forever mindful that many were former military men who were unable to adjust to civilian life.

Yet he tended to feel far more at ease talking to *The Big Issue* sellers, beggars and rough sleepers than to stockbrokers, bank clerks or insurance executives.

However, Frank had not lost his desire to be smartly turned out at all times, and this especially applied to the day he was due to meet his wife.

With this in mind, he quickly folded up his tent, packed and headed for the town centre toilets, where he could wash, shave and change into clothes that had been cleaned, pressed, folded and made ready to put on in advance.

Once he had changed, he walked to the Guildhall, in the Market Square, where his bike was parked. As always, beggars, buskers, *The Big Issue* sellers and rough sleepers sitting or lying near doorways were in evidence and largely ignored by passers-by.

As he approached the cycle racks, he almost collided with a fair-haired young man in a leather jacket and with a steely gaze.

"Excuse me, I wasn't looking where I was going," the young man said with a pronounced lisp. He was aged about thirty, just under 6ft tall, broad-shouldered and sun-tanned. He was clearly not an office worker or someone living on the edge, or a market trader, for that matter.

"That's all right, no problem," Frank replied, though he had a feeling it was a reply lacking in conviction.

Frank's first port of call that day was Laura's home in Richmond Road, near Cambridge's northern outskirts, where she lived with her new husband Peter. He could see straight away that the location was salubrious, though not exclusive, and that the street, accessed via the busy Huntingdon Road, consisted of a variety of well-established properties. Laura's home was about halfway along. The time was 10.30am, and Frank had ensured that he was neither too early nor too late.

A tall, trim-looking man, aged about fifty and with a full head of silvery grey hair and a military bearing, opened the door. "Good morning, I'm Peter Andrews," he announced. "You must be Frank Pugsley."

"Yes, I'm Frank."

The two men eyed each other for a few seconds, but in a speculative sense rather than in an adversarial stare-down.

"Do come in," Peter said. Then, on seeing Frank

hesitate, he suggested walking round the side of the house instead and having tea in the back garden. The garden was well manicured, being largely laid to lawn with carefully prepared flowerbeds to the side. A table laden with cups, plates, cakes and biscuits, plus three chairs stood in readiness.

"Do you like our garden?" Laura asked as she approached from the back of the house. "Gardening is my passion these days."

She was now forty, and Frank could see that, at last, she was beginning to look her age. The long, black hair was greying, the face strained and slightly lined, and those exquisite dark eyes had lost some of their lustre. But she still wore a pair of jeans well, her figure was trim and Frank still felt she was beautiful.

"This is my life now," she said with a wave towards the plants. "As I believe you know, Peter was a captain in the RAF before deciding to call it a day, and we now run a small travel agency together."

"I was a captain, too," Frank said to Peter with a half-smile.

The two men exchanged a few pleasantries about life in the armed forces, before Laura cut in. "You weren't at the funeral," she said curtly. "That was three months ago. Why are you here now?"

Peter put a comforting arm round her, as Frank squirmed.

"I'm really sorry," said Frank. "My head was all over the place. I want things to change. I want to change myself."

"It's a pity you didn't feel that way during the three years you weren't around. Terry needed a father. If you'd been there for him, things might have been different." The tone was in sorrow rather than anger.

"I know, I know. I can't put the clocks back, but I want to do something. I want to see if there is some way I can make things right."

"How are you going to do that? Terry's dead! He was just fifteen!" Laura was close to tears.

"What did you have in mind?" Peter asked Frank. Peter's tone could have been hostile, and Frank was relieved that it wasn't.

"I understand Terry died of a massive drugs overdose," said Frank. "Do you have any details of what occurred?"

"All we know is that he collapsed and died in a little road near Midsummer Common called Fair Street," Laura said. "He started to go off the rails when he was twelve… that's around the time you decided putting on a uniform and shooting people was more important than your family and walked out of his life. He got into bad company and, by the time he died, he had become an addict."

"Where was he getting the stuff from?"

"That's something the police would like to know," said Peter. "All we know is that there was a character called Toby involved."

"This Toby person, or whatever his real name is, would be on the phone to speak to Terry from time to time," said Laura. "We never met him, of course, and the police say they have never heard of anyone called Toby."

"Are the police still interested in the case?"

"They say they are keeping the case on file, whatever that means, but drugs are a big problem in Cambridge and, for the police, the death of Terry, is just another unsolved mystery, I'm afraid," said Peter.

Frank began to sense that a trigger could go off in his head any second. He rose to his feet and gave an involuntary roar. "Well, I'm not satisfied and I won't rest until I get to the bottom of this!"

As he made to leave, Laura shook her head. "What you need to do first is get yourself sorted out. You really do!" she said sadly.

Peter walked with Frank to the front gate and, with a knowing air, wished him the best of luck with his mission. "Let us know if we can help," he added.

Frank voiced thanks and headed towards the city centre, filled with the sort of resolution he had not experienced since the day he led an assault on an Iraqi stronghold and lost half a battalion during a successful but bloody battle.

He peddled back towards the city centre and then to Mill Road to meet Adrian and Germaine. Adrian had seen action in and temporarily suffered from shell shock during the first Iraq War, and the two men inevitably liked to compare notes on their experiences. Frank had originally met the couple in Bristol. Their home was a van, and, until now, they had rarely stayed in one spot for more than a few weeks.

However, Adrian was currently seeking treatment for alcohol addiction and, because they had stayed in Cambridge for the last three months, they had established something that remotely resembled roots.

The van was parked on a piece of wasteland close

to the railway bridge, and Germaine had undertaken to take charge of a large suitcase containing belongings that would not fit into Frank's backpack.

As usual, the meeting began with a game of chess, which Adrian won hands down. After that, the couple gave Frank a few tips on where best to camp. Frank felt more at home in the couple's company than just about anyone else.

"Drug dealing and addiction are rife in Cambridge and the police seem to be unable to cope," Germaine said.

"Does the name 'Toby' mean anything to you?" Frank asked.

The couple looked at each other and shook their heads.

"We've heard that drugs are big business in the city and that there's a local gang who have it all sewn up," said Adrian. "From what little I've heard, they're not the sort of people you want to tangle with."

"Do you know any names?"

"No, but there's a *Big Issue* seller who operates in the city centre and seems to have his ear permanently to the ground. If anyone knows anything, he will. He might even know who Toby is."

"Can you introduce us?"

"I can, but not today. Germaine and I have an AA meeting to go to, but you don't really need us. The guy's name is Billy Newton. He has thick, black hair and operates in St Andrew's Street, near Boots. And he always jokingly invites passers-by to join the shortest queue in Cambridge! All you need to do is buy a magazine, give him my name and you're in!"

The loquacious Billy was not hard to find, not even during the lunchtime rush. His call to join the 'shortest queue' could even be heard above the singing of buskers, the traffic and the hubbub of shoppers.

"You've found him," Billy said, on being approached. "And I reckon I know who you are. You're Frank Pugsley! Right?

"Strewth, how do you know that?"

"Elementary, my dear Pugsley!" Word has a way of getting around, and there's not much that gets past me!" Billy replied, with more than a little pride. "You're the bloke who sorted out Rick O'Reilly, who's none too popular, and you've become something of a celebrity!"

"What about Toby? Have you heard of a drugs dealer called 'Toby'?"

Billy paused for a moment and then chuckled. "His real name is Oliver Tobias Fretwell, which I think you will agree is a bit of a mouthful. So everyone calls him Toby."

"I would like to meet him. Is he big in the drugs scene?"

"No, not really. He fancies himself as a major player, but he's really just one of a number of dealers, probably an addict himself, who's run by Tommy Morris. Now there's someone you don't want to get on the wrong side of. And rumour has it that there's someone even higher up in the chain than Morris."

"Any idea who?"

"I have an idea, but that's all it is. There's a local letting agent by the name of Radford, who owns various properties in and around Cambridge and is said to be involved in all sorts of sleazy activities such as charging extortionate rents, organising seedy parties and arranging dodgy deals with local businessmen. No one's been able to link him with the Cambridge drugs scene though, and in any case, it's just a rumour."

"Hmm, any idea where I might find this Toby character?"

"Yes, he usually hangs around the Victoria Avenue area and can sometimes be seen in the Fort St George. He's short and stocky with curly blond hair. I'm not sure you will get much out of him. He's a bit of a thicky, to be honest."

"Thanks all the same. You've been very helpful," said Frank.

As Frank turned to collect his bicycle and head for the 'Fort', Billy tapped him on the shoulder.

"I must give you a word of warning," he said. "Tommy Morris and his associates are not to be trifled with. They are dangerous. They have the local drugs scene sewn up and even the dealers who try to muscle in from London know better than to mess with them."

"I'll watch it," said Frank, "but there's something I have to find out."

"I know you do, and don't think that I don't sympathise," Billy replied.

As Frank made his way to the Guildhall cycle rack, he nearly collided with the fair-haired man in the leather jacket again. But this time the latter sidestepped neatly and no words were exchanged.

But as Frank started to cycle away, he just had time to see the man sidle up to a startled-looking Billy and say something to him. Frank could not hear, but, being an adept lip-reader, he did not need to.

"I hope you haven't been shooting your mouth off again," were the words, and Billy bore the look of someone who dearly wished he hadn't.

The man who had caused such consternation had to be Tommy Morris, Frank concluded.

CHAPTER 3

Tracking down Toby turned out to be a far from easy task. He was not at the Fort St George and, when Frank made enquiries, it looked as if he had not been there all day. Frank could see no sign of anyone fitting his description on Midsummer Common either.

So, when it became apparent that the initial search was going to be fruitless, the logical next step was to find somewhere to camp for the night. Taking note of the recommendations made by Adrian and Germaine, Frank found another spot on Stourbridge Common that was further along than where he was the previous night. The location was near the footbridge and a hedge, and was far more secluded.

His mind raced as he lay on his bed. The meeting with Laura had been a disappointment. There were still things remaining to be said, Frank felt, and the thought that there was little or no hope of reconciliation depressed him. Laura had hardly greeted him like the Prodigal Son, and there appeared to be little doubt that she was committed to Peter. Yet none of this altered the fact that there was much that he wanted to say to her. It was just a matter of working out what!

However, on the plus side, Frank had found his encounter with Peter heartening. It could so easily have been acrimonious. Yet instead, and probably because of the military connection, there had been something approaching rapport. Peter had even offered to help and he sounded as if he meant it.

Frank's mind then turned to a meeting the next day for lunch he had arranged with Stephanie, who was going to be off duty that day. That was food for thought, too.

After a night's sleep that easily surpassed the one of the previous night, Frank focused once more on the question of finding Toby. After cycling back to the Fort, he trawled Midsummer Common in its entirety before twice going up and down Victoria Avenue, which accessed the Fort and led to Mitcham's Corner, and then he covered the whole of Jesus Green. After that, he tried some of the nearby pubs, such as the Old Spring and the various hostelries that could be found along King Street. Still no joy.

The search would have to be resumed after lunch.

Stephanie Shawcross was bang on time. Frank, who had been standing outside the gate to the Fort St George a couple of minutes earlier, saw her tie her bicycle to the roadside railings nearby and stride purposefully towards him. She was modestly clad in a dark trouser suit and lace-up shoes, though her buttercup blonde hair had been allowed to drop down to her shoulders and she wore a beaming smile.

"I would imagine you would prefer to eat outside," she said.

19

"I always prefer to be outside, though with you I could make an exception!" Frank quipped.

"So that's settled then," Stephanie said without hesitation as she walked towards a table that overlooked the river. The only noticeable reaction to the quip was a slightly arched eyebrow.

"How are you feeling now, Mr Pugsley?" she asked after she and Frank had sat down and ordered.

"I'm fine, as long as you call me Frank."

"No problem! And you can call me Steph," the WPC said as she took off her jacket to reveal a blouse and strong, sturdy arms.

Frank could not get away from the thought that, although she had no claim to beauty, she was far from unattractive.

"Have you always been a policewoman?" he asked.

"Pretty much, though not for long," said Steph. "I took a degree in criminology and then worked at Marks & Spencer until my exam results came out and while my application to join the police was going through. I've never really wanted to do anything else. I have always liked to read crime reports in the newspapers and frequently imagined myself as an ace detective since I was knee-high to a grasshopper. I have always liked being out of doors, too, and have always been into sports including judo. One thing is for sure. The idea of spending a lifetime working in an office doesn't appeal at all!"

"Something tells me you would rather be in plain clothes than in uniform one day."

Steph nodded.

"Is drugs-busting on your radar, by any chance?"

The hint of vehemence in Frank's tone was not lost on Steph.

"It certainly is. Drugs are a big problem in Cambridge, as I'm sure you're well aware. I haven't been around for long enough to know all the ins and outs of what's going on, but there does seem to be an organised gang that controls virtually all the movement and dealing in drugs here, and anyone who challenges them is wiped out. We can't prove this, we just pretty much know."

"So you have no idea who's running things?"

Steph sighed. "Yes, we do have ideas but no evidence. We manage to arrest dealers from time to time, but the ones we get are just small fry. They are usually addicts themselves, and they either don't know who the Mr Big is or are too afraid to give us a name."

Frank's eyes narrowed. "Why don't you give me a name or two?" he urged. "You will have worked out by now that I move in some interesting circles. I might just be able to win the trust of one or two people who would not trust the police. Give me a name or two, for me to work on, and you could end up with all the credit from the resulting arrests. It could lead to a commendation, perhaps even stripes."

Frank refrained from naming names himself because he was not sure at this stage if he should let on what he knew already. It did not amount to much, in any case.

"It could also land me in a heap of trouble," said Steph.

"Well, at least think about it!" Frank's face was now crimson, and his eyes resembled burning embers.

Steph felt the need to find safer ground, and so she adroitly changed the subject.

"You were expressing interest in my background," she

said, trying to sound casual. "Have you worked out that I hail from Devon?"

"Er yes, I have and I should imagine you know of my West Country origins?"

"Yes, you've already told me where you've come from, and Pugsley is a good, old-fashioned Bristol name."

Frank told Steph about his meeting with Laura and Peter and Steph offered Frank a brief insight into life at the local nick.

"They're a good lot on the whole, though one or two of the blokes are a bit chauvinistic and I don't go a bundle on a certain Inspector Wainwright, who happens to be in charge of drugs-busting," she said. "He's a bit of a lazy sod and spends most of the time out on the piss... if you'll excuse my French!"

"Do you know anything about Toby or Oliver Tobias Fretwell, to give him his full name?"

Steph shook her head. "Sorry, Frank, can't help you with that one. But do bear in mind that I'm still little more than a rookie, and I haven't been in Cambridge for that long. I'd need to do some digging to find answers to some of your questions. Having said that, it wouldn't surprise me if that twat Wainwright didn't know anything either!"

Frank could not stop himself from smiling.

Then, just before he and Steph rose to go their separate ways, he asked without the hint of a smile: "Have you had time to think about giving me a name or names?"

Steph winced. "Oh, Frank!" she said sorrowfully. "That's a big ask! Let me sleep on it at least."

At this point, she put on her jacket, said she would be in touch and jogged athletically back to her bicycle.

Frank watched her cycle northwards towards her home, which he believed she said was in Milton, before turning his mind to the question of finding Toby.

He had learned quite a bit in a short time about a side of the prosperous University city he had visited that was little talked about outside it. He could see that much of Cambridge's 'underbelly' was ruled by one ruthless gang. But he was no closer to finding out who was responsible for Terry's death.

It was time to look for Toby again, and this time he spread his net a little wider. Apart from re-visiting the pubs he had already been to and trying some new ones, he began to quiz homeless people sitting near shop doorways and the *Big Issue* sellers. Unfortunately the loquacious Billy Newton, who seemed as likely as anyone to be willing to help, was nowhere to be seen. Three of the people he quizzed said they knew who Toby was, but had no idea of his whereabouts.

After a couple of fruitless hours, Frank decided to have a coffee somewhere and 'regroup'. He needed to work out what he had been doing wrong.

Then, as he approached the door of a coffee bar, a wizened old woman carrying a cello sidled up to him and asked: "Have you tried the Hopbine, in Fair Street?"

When Frank admitted he had not, the old woman said: "It's off Maids Causeway, on the right. It's difficult to find if you've never been there before, and I know Toby goes in there from time to time."

Frank voiced thanks and said he would go there straight away.

"Be careful," the lady said. "He's a nasty piece of work."

Frank saw Toby as soon as he opened the pub's main door. His quarry was sitting on his own at a table in the far corner, hunched over a racing magazine but not paying much attention to it.

As Frank approached, Toby got up, hurled the table at him and fled. The table was heavy and Frank was only able to partially avoid it.

Toby made the most of the head start he had given himself and shot across Maids Causeway and on to Midsummer Common. However, Frank caught up with him at a speed that put the fear of God into him.

"Don't run away from me, you toe rag!" Frank said through his teeth. "I want words with you!"

Toby pulled a screwdriver out of his top pocket, and Frank did not need to be told that it was not used to correct faulty joinery!

"Stay away from me, or I'll cut you!" Toby said with the air of a caged animal.

Toby lunged at Frank with his makeshift weapon before trying to kick, punch and head-butt him, but to no avail. Although he was of similar size, he was simply no match for an adversary who had a counter for any move he could try.

In the end, Toby sat down on the grass and burst into tears.

Frank stood over him for a few seconds before saying: "You know who I am, don't you? Don't you! I am your worst nightmare!" He slapped Toby's face hard. "You supplied my son with heroin, didn't you? Didn't you!" There was another slap. "He was just fifteen when he died of an overdose. You know that, don't you?" Two more slaps followed.

Toby wailed like a baby. "It wasn't just me," he pleaded. "There were others. I was just doing what I was told."

"Oh you were, were you? Who was doing the telling?"

"I can't say. If I do, they will kill me!"

"I will kill you if you don't!" said Frank, who hit Toby with a clenched fist. "Tell me now, or I will take you apart!"

"I work for Tommy Morris," said a sobbing Toby.

"That's not good enough! I've already worked that one out by myself. Who's Morris working for?" Frank raised his fist again. "Tell me!"

"Tony Radford."

"What, the property owner and letting agent? What does he do?"

"Please, please!" pleaded a quivering Toby. "I'm just a small player!"

"I've already worked that out as well!" said a snarling Frank. "Answer my questions or, God help me, I will kill you!"

"Radford and Morris do a lot of business together. Radford charges over-the-top rents and he uses Morris and his heavies to intimidate tenants and sometimes to force them out of their homes. Morris makes use of some of Radford's properties as places for doing drug deals and for punishing users who fall behind on payments."

"Is Radford in the drugs business himself?"

"I don't know, I honestly don't know."

"Then there must be someone else," said Frank. "Come on! Who?"

Toby went white. "I'm a dead man!" he wailed.

"You will be if you don't talk now!" Frank delivered another slap.

"I'm told that the man at the very top is a wealthy, well respected local businessman… a man who no one suspects and who always manages to keep his hands clean."

"I want a name! Give me a name!"

By now a small crowd had gathered, including a couple of homeless men whose interest in what was occurring was by no means purely academic.

In the distance, the siren of a police car could be heard.

A whimpering Toby took advantage of the diversion and fled.

CHAPTER 4

Tony Radford was unavailable and would be out for several hours, Frank was told when he called round to his main branch.

Apart from the up-market Hawkins, Radford's was the biggest and best-known firm of estate agents in town. Lettings formed the main part of Radford's business.

"He might be at one of our other offices, but I doubt it," the young woman at the front desk said. "He's usually making calls at this sort of time. Can anyone else help, or can I leave a message?"

"No, that's all right, thanks," said Frank. "It's personal."

As he left, he decided that, on reflection, he could do just as well, if not better, at this stage by having words with some of Terry's former contemporaries and schoolteachers, too, for that matter.

But, first of all, he needed to see Laura again. Apart from anything else, she would be better placed than anyone else to advise him on who might be best to talk to.

"So, at last you want to talk about Terry!" Laura said ironically. "Well, I suppose late is better than never even if he is dead." Laura regretted the barb straight away and apologised.

"That's all right," said Frank. "No doubt I deserved that."

The once love-struck couple gazed at each other from garden chairs. The love had dimmed, but, for Frank at least, the electricity was still there albeit at a lower voltage.

"Do you remember the day Terry went to his first school in Bristol at the age of four?" Laura asked at length. She could sense that Frank was taking a deep breath through his muscular chest.

"I remember the event in every detail," her former husband replied. "There's not much I don't remember, in fact... at least not much before he was eleven or twelve."

Frank gazed at Laura's jeans-clad legs and saw they were still shapely, before averting his eyes towards the grass below.

"I remember him doing well at school. He was especially good at sports, had lots of friends, and his classwork wasn't so bad either," he observed.

A pause followed, during which two faces blackened.

"Then came the move to Cambridge, and Terry had to make new friends," Frank said with a sigh.

"Yes, that's true, but things were reasonably good at first. Terry seemed to settle in well at his new school, he made new friends, and he always got on well with Peter. Peter was never a substitute father, of course... there never could be one... but at least there was none of the friction that could have occurred in such circumstances."

"Good for Peter," Frank murmured. "So what went wrong?"

"He got into the wrong crowd. You're always hearing about it happening with other people – but well, that's what happened." Laura forced back the tears. "There were three or four lads who used to call round to see Terry regularly, to go out and perhaps kick a football around, or just to hang out, but, after a while, they stopped calling. Instead there were regular phone calls from this character Toby. We never met him face to face, and he never said what he wanted to talk to Terry about."

Laura was almost sobbing. "Terry started to become thin and gaunt. He would disappear for hours in the evening, and we eventually learned he had been playing truant from school. Then, one evening, Peter and I decided to have a rummage in his bedroom, and we found a pipe, a cigarette lighter and an ashtray – all things that suggested he was on drugs. When we brought this up with Terry, he went berserk. He shouted, swore, slammed doors and threw crockery and furniture around the house."

"All totally out of character," Frank observed.

"Absolutely! He stormed out of the house and that was the last we saw of him alive. He stopped going to school altogether and the only clue we had to his whereabouts was a note from Terry saying he had gone to live with friends. The note was pushed through our letterbox a couple of days after he stormed out."

"What did his teachers have to say?"

"They more or less confirmed our worst fears. They said his behaviour had changed out of all recognition. The once easy-going lad who everyone liked and who did well in class and even better at sports had turned into a nightmare to handle. It was just like Jekyll and Hyde!"

"Did the teachers have any idea why?"

"Well, yes. A couple of drug dealers had been seen hanging around the front gates, and the headmaster issued a warning at assembly one morning that pupils should have nothing to do with them under any circumstances."

"And don't tell me. Not everyone took his advice?"

"That's about it," said Laura. "Mind you, everyone did apart from Terry and one other boy."

"Did the other boy get hooked on heroin, too? Do you know his name and how I can contact him?"

"Yes, his name's Brian Simmonds. He's one of those people whose heart's in the right place but is known as someone who has to do whatever it is that he is advised not to do. I can give you an address if you really think that will help."

"It might well do. It sounds as if he could have led Terry astray. Did he get hooked on heroin, too?"

"Yes, I believe he did. I know his parents were desperately worried about him, though I have had no contact with the family for several months."

"OK," Frank said through his teeth. "I will be having words with this Brian Simmonds, and with his parents, too, for that matter. I still want to know more about how Terry and his friends got their hands on drugs in the first place, and who from. And I don't just mean Toby. He's just a pawn."

"Oh, do be careful," pleaded Laura. "I know nothing about the Cambridge drugs scene at all, except that the people running it are reputed to be extremely nasty."

Frank detected a genuine concern for his wellbeing. He then asked about Terry's other friends, but was told that the few Laura knew about were now all living in other parts of the country. She was able to give him the name of Terry's final form teacher, though.

"Don't let your tea get cold," Laura then said in an attempt to lighten the mood.

Frank turned in his chair to study the lawns, flowerbeds filled with plants that were mostly in full bloom and the trees that stood either side of the garden and at the back. Some of the trees bore various kinds of fruit.

"I can see that life in the suburbs still suits you," he said.

Laura smiled and told Frank the tale of how, at the age of twelve, her family were living in a house with half an acre of rear garden in North Cheam, in Surrey, that contained a dozen or so plum trees.

"I quite like plums these days," she said. "But at the time they were total anathema to me.

"The house we lived in was a fairly nondescript semi, but what made most people sit up and take notice was the size of the garden and its plethora of plum trees. What this meant was that every single meal finished with plums. The only room for guesswork beforehand was the question of whether the plums for pudding were going to be red or yellow.

"When we weren't eating them, we were picking them off the branches or from the ground. Sometimes the plums were rotting, and this made me retch. Yet hour upon hour was spent gathering these infernal plums, putting them on trays and taking them into the kitchen for bottling. Mummy seemed to spend all her time doing that in

Cheam, and, when I wasn't at school or doing homework, I would be drafted in to help."

Frank had heard the tale more than once before. But, perhaps because suburbia was a hitherto unknown world to him, he never tired of hearing it.

"You can imagine my relief when we upped sticks and moved to the West Country," Laura concluded.

Frank was fuelled by a glow of animation he had not felt for years.

He could not resist the urge to relate to Laura the story of how the mythical Icarus dropped in on his life.

"He tried to fly to the sun," my short-term foster father told me. "But the heat of its rays melted the wax that stuck the wings to his arms, and when the wax fell off, he fell into the sea.

"There was a copy of the painting by Bruegel hanging in the living room. There was no garden to speak of, but I was six at the time and the painting, called *Landscape with the Fall of Icarus*, enthralled me.

"I spent hours looking at it. There were two tiny legs in the right hand corner. One leg was flat, the other pointing at forty-five degrees. The water in the corner was dark, almost black, compared with the azure blue of elsewhere. One area in the middle was bathed in sunlight, which also dominated the horizon. There were rocks, ships one just inches from the legs and other people, too.

"In the foreground atop a small cliff was a farmer behind an ox and plough. A little lower down, a shepherd surrounded by sheep was leaning on a crook. And, on the shoreline, again not far from the legs, was a man dipping an arm into the sea.

32

"Yet all three were unaware of, or impervious to, the mythical event"

Laura knew the story almost by heart, but could not bring herself to halt the flow.

It was at this point that Peter appeared.

"Hello, what's going on here?" he asked.

Frank sensed that the tone was far from adversarial and responded with the quip: "I'm trying to steal your wife!"

Before any sort of reaction was possible, Laura, who did not seriously expect one, said to Peter: "Have you had a good outing, darling?"

"Sure."

"I have been giving Frank what little information I have about whom Terry might have been associating with before he died.

Peter nodded, and said to Frank: "I meant what I said about offering to help."

Mrs Simmonds was a tall, thin woman with ginger hair and a care-worn face. She looked older than her forty years.

When Frank told her who he was, she invited him into the Victorian terraced house she occupied with her son in nearby Benson Street.

"You're not likely to find Brian here," she said wearily, "especially now that I've stopped giving him money for drugs and taking steps to ensure that he doesn't steal the cash I put aside for shopping."

Frank managed to make sympathetic noises. "I would like to talk to him, but, while I am here, I wonder if you could shed any light on what happened to my Terry. Did you know Terry?"

Mrs Simmonds confirmed that she did. "He seemed a nice, balanced lad, just like Brian was, until drug dealers started hanging around the gates of their school."

"Do you know any names?"

"Only a character called Toby, who is often on the phone asking for Brian… and Tommy Morris, whose name has been mentioned once in a while as the local hard man."

"What about Tony Radford?"

"I've heard the name. He's an estate agent who specialises in lettings. I'm told he has a particularly bad reputation."

"Do you know if Radford is involved in the drugs scene at all?"

"No, not that I've heard. That's the sort of thing that Terry, bless his heart, would have known. Come to think of it, I remember Terry once saying that the whole Cambridge drugs scene was controlled by a mysterious Mr Big."

"Perhaps that's Radford?"

"Possibly, though I really don't know. Terry might have known. He seemed to have a way of finding things out."

"Did he now!"

Mrs Simmonds suddenly looked desperately tired, as if burdened by all the world's ills, and rose from the chair where she was sitting and motioned Frank towards the front door.

"The best place to look for Brian is in the Mill Road area," she told him. "You might well find him lying on a bench in the cemetery."

When Frank asked to speak to Terry's teacher, or perhaps the school principal at Parkside Community College, he found that the principal, Ian Robertson, was happy to oblige.

"Your loss is something that deeply concerns us all," he said, as soon as Frank was comfortably seated in his study. "Is there anything I can do to help?"

"I want to find out what happened and, if it's at all possible, to nail the drug dealers," Frank said, after recounting briefly what he had been doing and what he had heard since his arrival in Cambridge.

The slightly built principal eyed him speculatively. "That could be a dangerous game, as I'm sure you realise," he said. "There's not much I can tell you that you don't know already."

"Fair enough," said Frank. "However, if there's anything else that occurs to you, anything at all, that you can pass on, I would appreciate it."

The principal paused for a moment, before saying: "One thing I do remember about Terry is that a few months before his death, he developed an interest in horseracing. He once got into a bit of trouble for trying to persuade some of his friends during class time to help him buy a horse, which he could then enter into races. I don't suppose that bit of information is of any use at all, but there it is for what it's worth."

The words of Laura, Mrs Simmonds and Ian Robertson raced around Frank's head as he walked across the asphalt playground towards the iron gates.

As he passed through the gates, he espied a familiar figure hovering outside.

"How's it going?" the fair-haired man in the leather jacket and sun-tanned complexion lisped.

"How's what going, and who the hell are you?" Frank replied curtly.

Tommy Morris chuckled. "All right, all right, have it your way! You don't know who I am! Let's just say I'm a local benefactor, the guardian of people's wellbeing in Cambridge. I make sure everyone stays in line and, if possible, stays healthy." Frank had never seen a pair of eyes that looked more like fists.

"I want to know what happened to my son Terry, what really happened and I don't need anyone to keep me in line," Frank snarled.

"Haven't you read the papers?" Tommy asked in feigned amazement. "The tragic event was recorded as death by misadventure."

"I know, and I'm not satisfied."

"Well, I rather fear you'll have to be. The case is closed. You should count your blessings… at least you're still alive!"

Frank realised this conversation was not getting him anywhere. "I don't take kindly to veiled threats and you can rest assured I haven't finished asking questions. No doubt I will be seeing you again soon!"

"Excellent!" his sneering antagonist replied. "You can find me most evenings between six and eight at Cambridge's mixed martial arts club. Pop in sometime. You might learn something!"

CHAPTER 5

F inding Brian Simmonds was the top priority of the day, Frank decided on waking. As the only contact of the same age as Terry and, hopefully the same wavelength, perhaps Brian could provide some input, some vestige of a clue that would go towards explaining Terry's death. Frank hoped the youngster would not be too far gone on heroin to help.

However, dawn had only just broken, all was silent and even the moorhens nestling on a nearby river bank were comatose.

Frank washed and shaved by the river before following his customary early morning routine of indulging in deep breathing and stretching exercises, star jumps, press-ups and a run of a mile or so. Next on the agenda was packing up the tent and other belongings and cycling into town to buy breakfast.

His plan, after that, was to seek out Brian in and around Mill Road before visiting the van where Adrian and Germaine lived and acquiring a change of clothes. He would keep an eye open for Toby, too.

Frank remembered being told that the Kelsey Kerridge

Sports Centre, where he could do workouts, was close to Mill Road as were the 'nick' and Steph, for that matter.

Frank cycled up and down Mill Road three times before turning into the gravelled lane that led to the cemetery. Initially he travelled on the path that led to another entrance facing Norfolk Street before turning full circle to the point where he started. Unlike in many cemeteries, where graves and tombstones, for the most part, lay in orderly lines, the Mill Road burial place featured a higgledy-piggledy mix of mounds, headstones and unofficial paths.

Dogs and their walkers appeared from various directions, sometimes from spots that could not be seen until they were stumbled on. Frank counted six dogs, all of different breeds, during his quest to locate Brian. None of the owners knew, or were ever likely to know anything about a teenager with a drugs problem.

A couple of unshaven, unkempt men of about thirty who sat on a bench with a dozen empty bottles at their feet and an alcohol-induced stare could not help either.

A second visit to the cemetery would clearly be necessary.

As Frank pedalled along Mill Road away from the city centre once more, he could see why locals referred to the road as the 'real Cambridge'. With its profusion of small shops that had managed to defy what passed as progress and retain their character when so many elsewhere had been unable to, or simply gone under, Mill Road had managed to keep its identity.

There were plenty of down and outs, too. Some sat in

or near shop doorways; others in small groups had taken over a couple of bus stops.

Frank could not help pondering over the fact that reports of a burgeoning British economy abounded while the number of rough sleepers across the country seemed to rise day by day.

Still no sign of Brian Simmonds.

Frank crossed the Mill Road bridge and looked to the left to see that the van occupied by Adrian and Germaine was still in the same spot. Germaine greeted him with a wave and a smile.

"Adrian's out just now, so there can be no chess this time," she said, tongue in cheek.

Frank expressed regret, but felt relief, as Adrian was once a county schools champion and far too good for him.

"I should imagine you're after a change of clothes by now. Perhaps I shouldn't stand too close to you!" Germaine quipped.

"Perhaps not, but I did make a point of washing my hands before coming here," a laughing Frank retorted.

Germaine pulled out a large suitcase from under a makeshift back seat, unzipped the case and, not without some pride, indicated that she had kept everything in apple pie order.

"I can tell you the best place to get a bath or shower and where you can change your clothes," she said in her most authoritative tone. The matronly role came naturally to her, and she enjoyed it. "Meanwhile, just help yourself to what you need."

Frank fished out some trousers, socks, underwear

and a shirt and towel, and asked where he could wash the clothes he was wearing.

"Don't worry about that, just get cleaned up and changed and bring the dirty clothes back to me."

Frank felt an inner glow. He recalled the day Adrian, in a rare sober moment at the time, told him how he met Germaine in London when she was just sixteen and had been sleeping rough in the streets for almost two years. Her father, an eminent barrister, had had no time for her and packed her off to boarding school at the earliest opportunity. Her mother, meanwhile, was conducting an affair with a younger man in a caravan at the end of the family's long garden. The father was never at home and when Germaine was not at school her mother left her to fend for herself.

Not surprisingly, Germaine was beside herself with misery. One day, she simply packed up the few belongings she possessed and left without telling anyone. Subsequent life on the streets was bleak, but she never felt any desire to return home.

Eventually she met Adrian and formed a bond with him. And, as Adrian was keen to point out, she was his rock. She was the one who got him to join Alcoholics Anonymous. They had now been together for twelve years.

"Bring back the dirty clothes straight away, won't you," she said to Frank as she stood before him, tall, thin, cheaply but neatly dressed and proud.

"You can count on that. Bless you," said Frank.

After bathing, changing and feeling, hopefully, more approachable, Frank popped into the Kelsey Kerridge Sports Centre to learn what facilities were available to him.

The centre included a weights room, squash courts and other rooms that could be used for various other activities. Among those was the mixed martial arts club that Tommy Morris had mentioned. The notice, giving brief details, served as a reminder that, sooner or later, there would be a full-on confrontation. He was well aware that it would be no walk in the park.

When he got back to the van, another unpalatable confrontation was in the offing. Adrian had returned, and this meant another thrashing at chess. After what passed for a game, Frank and Adrian chatted for a while about their respective experiences in Iraq. More importantly, Frank was delighted to hear that Adrian was still off the booze and regularly attending AA meetings.

"Stay with it," Frank said as he left. "I take my hat off to you."

Frank resumed his search for Brian for a while, but still to no avail. The one *Big Issue* seller he saw in Mill Road had no knowledge of his whereabouts, or that of Billy Newton either for that matter. The cemetery was deserted, save a pair of foreign language students sitting on a bench with sandwiches and talking animatedly in Portuguese. The only other signs of life were a few empty beer bottles and cans, a couple of drug users' needles and dog excrement that had not been properly cleared up.

When he called in at Parkside Police Station and asked if he could speak to WPC Shawcross, he was told she was on patrol in another part of the city.

The next morning, he was at the sports centre. Fortunately

he was able to produce written evidence that he was qualified to use the weights, and it was not long before he was in full flow. He began with the equivalent of a mile on a treadmill before performing a series of stretching exercises. While working with the weights, he was gratified to know that, despite a lack of recent practice, 250lb for the bench press was still within his compass.

After a shower and a soft drink, he cycled up and down Mill Road and round the cemetery yet again. Still no sign of Brian.

Feeling more than a little frustrated, he headed for the Market Square, where he could sit for a while and observe a slice of life.

As he approached Boots, he spotted Billy Newton. Billy saw him first and promptly disappeared through the store's nearest door... but not before Frank observed a swollen lip and a pronounced limp. He parked his bicycle and went into Boots, too, but the loquacious yet illusive Billy was nowhere to be seen.

Eventually he trudged towards the Market Square. As he did so, another *Big Issue* seller beetled through the doorway of WH Smith.

In the square itself, tourists speaking in every tongue except English sat at tables sipping drinks. Others meandered round the market or stood in groups to listen to the buskers. One, a ten-year-old vocalist, was singing 'Ave Maria' to perfection. Frank, who had on occasion watched *The X Factor* on a friend's television, could not help thinking that some of the Market Square warblers could knock Simon Cowell's 'fantastic' stars of the future into a cocked hat.

Cambridge University students tended to congregate

elsewhere. However, the punt touts, ferociously competing for trade, were out in force. So, too, were the down and outs, members of a breed that frequented the area the most, but were noticed the least.

Still no sign of Brian. Or of Toby, or Morris, for that matter.

Frank sat and watched the little but varied world that was the Market Square for a couple of hours before deciding to have one more try at finding Brian.

Twilight was beginning to descend on the Mill Road cemetery when Frank paid it his last visit of the day. The one remaining dog walker was on the point of leaving as he began to pedal round the periphery. Rough sleepers were conspicuously absent on this occasion, and the whole place seemed genuinely ghostly.

He had almost completed his second cycle round when at last he heard signs of life from the cemetery's remotest corner.

"So there you are!" a rough-sounding East Anglian voice could be heard. "At last!"

Frank heard the sound of a blow being struck, followed by a groan. He sped towards the spot to see a burly young man with close-cropped hair and heavy boots standing over the slight form of a youth with ginger hair.

He saw two kicks delivered, followed by the words: "You've fallen behind on your payments once too often and you don't seem to understand what happens if you fail to pay what you owe!"

A third kick landed in the youth's face and blood started to trickle onto the path. The burly thug stood back for a moment to admire his handiwork before resuming the beating.

He never got the chance.

Frank tore into the thug with a savage intensity. One well directed blow put an end to the thug's resistance, but Frank was in an incandescent rage and he continued to administer a merciless beating. Although his adversary was a head taller and at least two stone heavier, Frank shook him like a rag doll before using fists, thumbs, elbows and feet to cause the maximum possible pain.

The thug pleaded for mercy, but the beating continued until he lost consciousness.

The thug's young victim sat on the ground a few feet away, mesmerised, until the beating stopped. He cringed when he realised he could be the next focus of attention.

Frank took a deep breath. "Don't worry, I'm not going to hurt you. Believe me, that's the last thing I want to do." Frank took some more deep breaths and was relieved to see that the ginger-haired youth was no longer afraid. "You're Brian Simmonds, aren't you?"

"How did you know?"

"I'm Terry Pugsley's father. I've met your mother, and she's worried about you."

All Brian could say at this point was: "Oh!"

"It seems to me that your mother has reason to worry," Frank added.

"I know. I don't know what to do."

"Let's get you out of here for starters," said Frank. "Are you able to walk?"

"My ribs are a bit sore, but I'll manage."

"Good. The first thing I'm going to do is take you back

to your mother. You can have a good night's sleep there, and tomorrow we can work out what to do next."

"I don't know how to thank you," said Brian.

"I'm hoping you will do that by answering a few questions about Terry," Frank replied, with feeling. "But don't worry just now. We can leave that until you feel a bit more up to it."

CHAPTER 6

Getting the bruised Brian home was no easy task. It entailed leaving a bicycle chained to a lamppost in Mill Road and walking to a taxi rank in the city centre. Brian had pleaded with Frank not to involve the police, despite the pain he was to endure with every step. Without help from Frank, he would almost certainly have been unable to make it.

Eventually they found a cabby who took Frank and Brian to Benson Street.

An effusively grateful Mrs Simmonds immediately offered to drive Frank back to Mill Road so that he could retrieve his cycle.

When Frank called on the Simmonds household the following morning, he was regaled with offers of coffee, cake and biscuits.

"We've decided the best course of action is for Brian to leave town," Mrs Simmonds told Frank. "I have a brother living in Leicester, and he says he knows people who can help him with his drugs problem. He says he can stay with him and his wife for as long as he likes and that I can join them in Leicester, too, if I want to."

"That sounds like the ideal arrangement," agreed Frank. "Apart from anything else, he should be safe there."

"I've got him fixed up to see a doctor, who can check him over, and, once that's been done, I will be putting him on a train," Mrs Simmonds added.

"Do you mind if I ask Brian one or two questions first?"

"No, not at all. I'll get him to come downstairs."

Frank asked Brian how he was feeling, once he appeared.

"Much better now, thanks." He was now able to smile, and Frank could detect that the slightly built young man was high-spirited, full of humour and probably able to be just as cheeky as Terry was. It was hard not to imagine Terry and Brian as good friends and kindred spirits.

He asked the question nonetheless. "Were you and Terry good mates?"

"Yes, we became buddies almost as soon as he first came to the school," Brian replied.

"Did Terry have any other mates?"

"Yes, he was pretty popular. There was a group of four of us who used to always go around together. We all liked sport, especially football and cricket. We liked the same kind of music, we played cards together and we larked around together. Sometimes we got into trouble, though it was never anything serious."

"What happened to the other two lads?"

"Both of their families have left Cambridge, I'm afraid, though towards the end Terry and I were not seeing so much of them."

"Why was that?"

Brian looked away, and Frank immediately knew what his next question should be. "Was that when the drug dealers started appearing at the school gates?" he asked after a pause.

Brian blushed and nodded.

"And, don't tell me, you and Terry got drawn in and hooked, and the other two didn't want to know?"

Mrs Simmonds cut in. "Can we change the subject? The damage has been done and we now need to see what we can do to mend it."

Frank apologised.

"OK, perhaps I can ask just one more question. Did Terry associate with anyone else that you haven't mentioned, or did he have any other interests?

Brian shook his head and said: "I'm sorry, there's nothing else I can think of."

Then, just as Frank began to thank him for his help, Brian suddenly said: "Just a minute, there is one thing. Terry became mad keen on horseracing. He got the rest of us to join him at the races in Newmarket, and he even tried to get us to club together and buy a racehorse between us so that we could enter it into races."

"Were the rest of you interested?"

"Not really. I think one of our group, John Goode, said he would think about it, and Terry also tried to get some of the others in our class to come in."

"Did he succeed?"

"No. All he succeeded in was getting into trouble with the teachers for disrupting lessons!"

"Oh dear! I suppose Terry became discouraged in the end and had to give up?"

Brian began to answer in the affirmative, but then remembered something else. "I'm not sure, but I think he tried to get a job working in some stables in Newmarket," he said.

"Any idea who owned the stables? Asked Frank.

"Again, I'm not sure, but I think they were owned by a businessman in Cambridge. It could have been an estate agent."

"That's interesting!" interjected Mrs Simmonds. "I've heard that one of the city's biggest estate agents owns a string of racehorses, and that horses are more of a passion for him than houses!"

"Is that Tony Radford, by any chance?"

"I'm afraid I don't know," said Mrs Simmonds.

"All I can remember is Terry saying he was toffee-nosed and that he would consider employing him to do mucking out," said Brian.

"Did Terry take him up on that?"

"I don't know for sure, but I have a feeling he said he was going to," said Brian.

"Not to worry," said Frank. "It's probably not important, anyway."

Frank then asked exactly when Brian would be leaving for Leicester.

It was Mrs Simmonds' turn to speak. "We are virtually packed and ready to go. I will join Brian in a day or two and we shall stay there until a programme to help Brian with his addiction has at least been put in place and starting to run."

Frank nodded his approval. "I have a feeling that the sooner you both go the better," he said, as he made to leave.

Next on Frank's agenda was a call to the nearby Richmond Road to tell Laura and Peter about his talk with Brian and his mother. However, they were both out, and so Frank left them a short note about his visit to the Simmonds' house and a promise to provide an update later.

This was followed by another workout at the sports centre, which, this time, incorporated a thirty-length swim.

After that, it was another visit to the 'nick' to see if Steph was available, though he was unsure whether the purpose was purely to extract information or something else. Again, no joy.

Frank pondered for a while over whether it was best to look up Adrian and Germaine again next, or to pop round to Radford's once more.

In the end, he decided to make his way to the Market Square and its surrounding streets, which had the biggest concentration of *Big Issue* sellers and more than its share of rough sleepers. He knew that many homeless people were drug addicts, too, and felt there was an outside chance of one of them being prepared, or able to provide some information, or give him a lead.

Frank was particularly keen to catch up with Billy Newton and try to find out why Billy had been so anxious to avoid him. He also wanted to locate Toby again, though no one seemed to know where he had got to.

As he approached the square, he saw the wizened old woman outside a shop strumming her almost silent cello.

"Be careful," the woman said, looking up. "You need to watch your step." Frank asked her what she meant, but she refused to be drawn and resumed her strumming.

A *Big Issue* seller gave Frank a knowing look and said: "I think Billy might be prepared to talk to you now."

A portly market trader trying to sell tawdry souvenirs eyed Frank in similar fashion. "Billy will talk to you now, but watch yourself. I hear there are people out to get you," he warned.

As Frank approached Boots, another *Big Issue* seller sidled up to him and said: "Billy will meet you in Pret à Manger – not the bigger one, but the smaller one in Petty Cury – in fifteen minutes."

"How are you feeling now?" Frank asked after buying a coffee from a Spanish girl at the counter at the far end and joining Billy Newton at a table for two a few feet away from the counter. The tables at Pret à Manger were all the same size, in two long lines, and they saw plenty of comings and goings.

"How do you know?" Billy replied, as he rubbed one side of his ribcage.

"Oh, I know all right! Who did it? Was it Morris, or did he get one of his sidekicks to do it?"

"It was Morris. He often farms out duffing-up jobs, but, now and again, he likes to do it himself. He gave me what he called a 'friendly thumping', saying I would need to lie down for a couple of days but should be able to be up and about after that. He says he administers some of the beatings personally to show others how it is done! But if you believe that, you will believe anything!"

"How do you know that sort of stuff?" Frank was both surprised and curious.

Billy managed a lopsided grin. "I guess it's because I

talk too much. As you have doubtless guessed by now, it sometimes gets me into trouble! I've always been someone who'll talk to anyone and everyone, and that means a lot of people talk to me and I find out things. I know rich men, poor men, beggar men and thieves – not to mention villains!"

"So did Morris beat you up for talking to me?"

Billy nodded.

"So why are you talking to me now? You went out of your way to avoid me the last time we saw each other, so why now?"

Billy's eyes flashed. "Because I heard about the way you sorted out Bart Bainbridge. That's the bloke who was knocking the hell out of Brian Simmonds until you stepped in. Brian's a nice kid, far too young to be caught up in the sort of scenario we are talking about – and I decided to hell with it!"

"Was Morris behind the attack on Brian?"

"Almost certainly. He has virtually the whole drugs scene sewn up in Cambridge. *Big Issue* sellers know it, welfare officers know it, and so do the police. But no one can prove it."

"And presumably the people most in the know are too afraid to say anything?"

"Absolutely! Morris heads up a bunch of about eight local heavies, who call themselves The X Factor and they're even more ghastly than that TV programme! Drug dealers, some of them addicts themselves of course, take their orders from The X Factor, and no one dares to defy them."

"Does this Bainbridge character belong to The X Factor?"

"No. I don't think so, though I believe he has ambitions in that direction," said Billy. "I think he wants to belong, but they won't take anyone!"

"It sounds as if beating up a late-paying drug user is just a routine job!"

"That's pretty much right. As you probably know, a dealer, who will do everything he can to exert power over an addict, or potential addict, will often let the addict fall behind on his or her payments. Then, when the addict has absolutely no chance of meeting that payment, the dealer will force the addict to commit a crime, or perhaps sleep with him to wipe the slate clean as an alternative to a beating. The beating can be pretty severe, and when I heard about the way you dealt with Bainbridge it, well, struck a chord with me."

Frank expressed both gratitude and concern over the fact that Billy was putting himself at risk.

"That's all right," Billy replied, vehemently. "The pain in my ribs is pretty bad, but it's nothing compared with the anger I feel about what's going on. A lot of other *Big Issue* sellers feel the same, and so do quite a few of the rough sleepers. If you can put a spoke in Morris's wheel, that's fine with me!"

Frank assured Billy he would do his best. "There is just one question, though," he said.

"Fire away!"

"Does Morris have a connection with the letting agent Tony Radford or anyone else in the Cambridge business community?"

Billy pondered for a moment. "I've heard something about him having an arrangement with one or two estate agents in Cambridge, but I don't know any details. I've heard that Radford has a habit of charging extortionate rents and even intimidating tenants, but I've never heard about him being involved with drugs."

"Never mind," said Frank. "You've told me plenty, and I appreciate it. We must keep in touch. Look out for yourself, though, won't you?"

"I certainly will," said Billy, extending a hand. "But you need to do the same. One way or another, I can smell trouble brewing!"

Before going to collect his bicycle from outside the Guildhall, Frank headed for WH Smith, in Market Street, to buy a newspaper.

It was not until he had paid for it and got outside that he saw the headline on the front page. It read:

BODY FOUND FLOATING IN CAM.

CHAPTER 7

There was no doubt in Frank's mind whose body it was. The report said that the man found dead in the Cam was aged around 25-30, 5ft 6in tall, of stocky build and with curly blond hair.

Nothing was said about the cause of death, though Frank was pretty certain that, whatever method had been used, Toby had been murdered in the interests of silence.

He wondered whether Billy or any of the other *Big Issue* sellers knew anything about this, or whether anyone such as the portly market trader who had told him that Billy was willing to talk, or the wizened old woman with the cello, or any of the rough sleepers could tell him anything. Or the police, for that matter.

Frank felt sceptical about the police being likely to know and even more so about the establishment generally. Yet, at the same time, it appeared that a local businessman... an establishment figure... might have been involved in some way.

He began to fear for the safety of people he had been in contact with. If Morris had been behind the killing of Toby, would the same fate befall Billy? Would Adrian and

Germaine, who would be vulnerable in their van, be safe? Or the woman with the cello? Or the other *Big Issue* seller? Or Laura and Peter?

The thought that the woman he still loved could be a victim of the predatory Morris was unbearable.

It was a thought that touched the trigger that was a constant source of fear for Frank. His hands automatically went up to his ears in a vain attempt to block out the demonic voice that repeatedly said, "Kill! Kill!"

Fortunately he had the foresight to stop cycling and dismount. He was approaching Midsummer Common, an open space that spelt salvation, but his next action was to lean his bicycle against a wall in readiness for potential flashing images. The one he dreaded most was the reminder of the time he saw two suspected snipers appear on a first floor balcony and shot them. It happened in Baghdad and the so-called assailants turned out to be an unarmed woman and a small child. Exoneration was instant, but the experience lingered unforgivingly.

On this occasion, Frank was spared. He took a series of deep breaths before walking with his bicycle towards Maids Causeway and then the common. The voice stopped and, not for the first time, Frank felt the immense relief of not being hemmed in. After a few minutes, he was able to cycle again.

However, as he headed towards the spot where he planned to camp for the next night, a new thought crossed his mind: What about his own safety? He had been warned that there were people out to get him, and he now cursed himself for failing to consider the danger earlier. From now on, precautions would be needed especially after dark.

The first prudent step, he decided was to find somewhere different to camp, in case his previous places of sleep were already known to his enemies. The second priority was to be hidden or at least hard to track down at night, and third was to avoid being cornered with no means of escape.

Achieving these objectives in a location that was as flat as a pancake and with little in the way of woodland to offer concealment, was no easy task.

Frank considered camping several miles outside Cambridge, but he decided against this as this would entail being isolated and out on a limb with no potential help at hand, if needed.

So instead, he plumped for a spot in the city's Chesterton area that was close to a riverbank and to another footbridge that led to a road. He pitched his tent on ground that was slightly sunken and beside a bush. The spot was far from perfect, but Frank was confident he could at least see nearby comings and goings and, most importantly, anyone approaching from a distance.

As always, he ensured that the zip down one side of his sleeping bag could be opened and closed quickly. A small baseball bat and a pepper pot lay within easy reach. Frank was not unused to dealing with unwelcome visitors, though, more often than not, they had been drunken revellers who had lost their way and needed directions. On other occasions, potential intruders had been frightened away by the sight of Frank emerging from under canvas with a baseball bat in his hand. The one person who had actually attacked him, as he lay apparently defenceless, was an escapee from Broadmoor who ended up begging for mercy after being sprayed with pepper and belaboured with bat.

Tommy Morris and his thugs could expect a warm reception!

At the very moment Frank was harbouring thoughts of what he would like to do to Morris, a sheet of lightning lit up the sky. A rumble of thunder followed, and for the next ten minutes hailstones gave the local terrain a pounding. Some of the stones were the size of golf balls, but Frank was secure in the knowledge that his tent was robust enough to withstand almost anything, bar cannon fire.

The storm ended as abruptly as it began, and Frank sensed that he was experiencing a lull before a storm of a different kind.

He did not have to wait long to be proved right.

After less than half an hour, the sound of what could have been a cavalcade of electric lawnmowers, had it been daytime, could be heard from afar. The sound soon became louder and Frank realised that motorbikes were approaching. Before long, four massive machines, possibly Harley Davidsons, came into view and stopped about fifty feet away. Four riders wearing balaclava helmets dismounted, spread out and approached. They were each carrying a baseball bat.

In the absence of an immediate escape route, Frank stood in front of his tent with his own bat and a pepper pot at the ready.

The four masked bikers, all over 6ft tall and employing a pincer movement, walked slowly and stealthily until they were about twelve feet away. Then, suddenly, they moved at the double and launched their assault.

One attacker, who was just a fraction ahead of the others, screamed as a stream of pepper found its way through the slit near his eyes, and was then felled by a blow from Frank's bat.

However, almost simultaneously, a blow to the head from a second biker knocked Frank to the ground. A boot sank into his side. Yet Frank was somehow able to get to his feet and deliver a kick that landed on a kneecap so hard that the sound of a bone breaking was unmistakable. The injured biker fell to the ground, writhing and screaming.

At the same time, another blow from a bat landed on Frank's shoulder. This was followed by another that hit the left side of his ribcage. The assailant who had had pepper thrown into his face had re-joined the fray, and so Frank was facing odds of three to one.

He was experienced enough in combat to know that he was hurt already and that escape was the course of action to take if at all possible.

He aimed a kick at another assailant's knee, but this time the kick did not land cleanly, and he had to take a kick that just missed his groin, himself.

The three bikers, who were clearly gaining the upper hand, then fell for a ploy born out of desperation and totally lacking in originality. When Frank looked slightly to the left and called out, "Over here, George!" there was enough of a distraction for him to flee towards the footbridge and the road. The road led to a busier road that saw activity all round the clock, and hopefully, the presence of people and an all-night café would be enough to deter his tormentors.

But the three bikers were not that easily denied. They caught up with Frank, whose mobility had been hampered by blows already received, and laid into him. Frank felled one of them with a well-executed left hook, but the other two felled him and then went to work with bats and boots as he lay on the ground. Frank curled himself into a ball to shield his face and groin. Yet the thump, thump, thump to various parts of his body seemed interminable, until a voice saying, "Right, let's get out of here," could be heard.

Frank could hear the sound of pounding boots as his assailants made their way back to their motorcycles.

He then heard a more familiar voice. On looking up, he saw Peter standing by his car and holding out a hand.

"Are you able to get up?" Peter asked.

Frank did exactly that and promptly passed out.

CHAPTER 8

"TODAY'S YOUR LUCKY day," Tommy Morris lisped. As always, the lisp was at its most pronounced when he was at his most menacing.

The dishevelled wreck of a man kneeling at his feet looked up from the floor for a moment.

"I've got a little job for you to do," Morris told him. "If you do it well, I might just accept it as payment in kind! Perhaps even payment in full! When you've done it, and if I'm in a good mood, I might even give you some stuff for free. How does that sound to you?"

The addict continued to look at the floor of the remote lock-up garage to which he had been taken.

The man standing behind slapped the addict's head and ordered him to answer.

"What do you want me to do?" the addict asked.

"That's not good enough! Show some gratitude!" the man behind him said as he delivered another slap.

Tommy Morris tittered. "All right, all right, I can see you're dying to find out what I have in mind. Aren't you?"

"Yes, Mr Morris."

"Excellent! The job I want you to do is to dig a hole.

Not for yourself this time, but for me!" The man standing behind ensured that he echoed his boss's laughter.

"What I want you to do," Morris continued, "is dig a big, deep hole in front of a house in Hopper Street, which is on Cambridge's northern outskirts. It needs to be done tonight. Bart here will drive you there, and he will provide you with a pickaxe to break up the concrete and a spade for digging the hole. The hole has to be wide and deep, and it must be exactly up to, and in front of the front door. Do you understand?"

"Yes, Mr Morris."

"Bart will show you exactly where to dig and then you will be on your own, though Bart will come back at regular intervals to make sure you're doing the job properly. He will drive you back to the city centre once it's been done and the job has to be finished by first thing in the morning. Understand?"

The addict nodded.

"Good! Then it should be a good day for all of us. Apart from being good for you, it will be good for our friend Bart here, who's trying to earn his spurs as a member of The X Factor. And, you never know, I might be a happy bunny, too!"

"How did you do it?" Lee Bains asked in his thick, Norfolk accent. "How on earth did you manage to swing it?"

Tony Radford grinned. "I could ask the same of you. How did you manage to come up with the money?"

The two men had a fair idea of the answers to their questions already.

Bains grinned, too. "I guess we've got a bit of a mutual admiration society here!"

Bob Wainwright and the other guests looked at the pair quizzically.

"How's our mutual friend, Janice?" Radford asked.

Janice Seagrave ran a small estate agency in the Suffolk town of Haverhill. Lee Bains had walked into her office and into her life one day and, before long, they were having a full-blown affair. The couple had decided to form a business partnership, and one of the first steps to this end was for Janice to transfer £30,000 from her bank account into a special 'Development Account', which happened to be in her lover's name.

"She's a sweetheart!" said Bains. She's great in bed, too!" Then he added with a sneer: "And, luckily for me, all her brains are downstairs!"

Tony Radford laughed.

Bob Wainwright said, tongue in cheek, that he did not know what the property developer meant.

Then, as Wainwright finished off his glass of wine and looked for where he could refill it, Bains asked Radford: "How did you persuade that Jones woman to change her mind about staying put, after all this time? I thought there was no way we would ever get rid of her!"

"It's a bit of a mystery, really," Radford responded. "Mrs Jones had been away at her son and daughter-in-law's at the weekend, and when she returned she found there was a huge hole right in front of her front door."

"Making access to her home impossible, presumably?"

Radford could not resist a smirk. "That's about the size of it. And the silly cow suddenly decided she was better off living with relatives than being on her own, after all."

"She's getting on a bit, isn't she?"

"Yes, she's in her late eighties, if not her nineties. Time for her to go, I'd say. Wouldn't you?"

"Yes, of course it is. Silly old bags like her shouldn't be allowed to stand in the way of progress!"

Lee Bains and Tony Radford exchanged approving glances and moved to the drinks table, where they could further fuel their feelings of self-satisfaction.

The former could, at last, go to work on the small row of Hopper Street houses, which were now all empty, while the latter could make a killing by marketing a brand new Bains development.

The party was taking place in the lounge of an up-market house that Tony Radford had been instructed to sell. The vendor, whose main home was in Northumberland, was not present to question the agent's methods, which could euphemistically be described as unorthodox.

Guests at the party included Sam, a nephew and protégé of Tony Radford, Radford's secretary Maisie and three other women clad in vests, hot pants and high-heeled shoes, who sat in a row of upright chairs and gazed forlornly into space. One was in her forties and the other two in their twenties, and they had been kitted out by the matriarchal Maisie.

Bob Wainwright leered at the trio from across the room. "I fancy the slim, leggy one," he whispered to his host.

"So do I," declared Sam.

Tony Radford sighed. "Sorry, gentlemen, but I think she's booked. You Know Who has first choice."

"So I suppose we will just have to wait until he arrives!" Sam said a mite indignantly.

"'fraid so!"

Bob Wainwright chuckled. "Not to worry! Let's not be impatient! I'm perfectly happy to wait, and, even if neither of us gets the one we want, the other two aren't so bad, are they?"

The burly police inspector, who took pride in his capacity to down massive quantities of alcohol and in his middle age spread, poured himself another glass of claret and downed it without bothering with such niceties as taste.

"I see you've been admiring the… er… talent," Maisie said as she walked up to him.

"That's very perceptive of you, you ought to be in the police!" the inspector replied.

The tall, broad-shouldered Maisie ran a hand through her peroxide blonde hair and gave a throaty laugh. "I'm happy where I am. You might have your perks, but so do I!"

Her voice was almost drowned by the sudden sound of music from a loudspeaker.

"Right, ladies and gentlemen, it's time for a bit of music and dancing," Tony Radford announced. "Don't be shy, gentlemen. We've got three nice little fillies here to keep you amused!" He pointed to the trio seated in a row along a wall.

Maisie gestured to the three women to get up and gyrate. Bob Wainwright joined them and, after a few moments, so did Sam. The others sipped their drinks and urged the women to keep shaking their booty.

The music became louder, the drinks continued to flow and the dancing became increasingly frenetic.

There was a loud cheer when strains of 'The Stripper' could be heard. Bob Wainwright began to unbutton his shirt. The slim, leggy girl retreated to her chair… only to be hauled to her feet by Maisie and ordered to join in.

"Get 'em off!" roared Lee Bains.

"That includes you, Bob!" shouted Tony Radford," and you!" he said to Sam.

The woman in her forties, who had seemed to know what to expect from the outset, shed her shoes and started to peel off her vest.

Bob Wainwright took off his shirt to reveal a powerful, if somewhat flabby torso. Sam disappeared. The leggy girl wanted to do the same, but could feel the force of Maisie's gimlet eye. The older woman displayed a figure that was far better preserved than Wainwright's, while the third girl, who was short and stocky, copied every move made by the older one.

After a few minutes, all the dancers were topless. Maisie glared at the leggy one as the latter adopted a cross-armed pose, and a roar went up as Wainwright began to remove his trousers.

Then the music stopped.

"Don't let me interrupt you!" said Tommy Morris, who had just walked in. "Don't let me stop you from having your fun!"

"Hi there, Tommy, good to see you!" said Tony Radford. "Let me tell you straight away that I've got a packet of fun in store for you!"

There was a nod of approval.

"Come and have a drink and let me introduce you to Lee Bains. You have, of course, met Bob, Maisie and Sam already." He filled a glass with chilled orange juice while Morris and Bains shook hands.

"Nice job you did the other day," he added as he handed the teetotal Tommy his drink.

"No problem! I believe there's some sort of payment in kind, anyway."

"Well, of course! As always! That's how we do business, isn't it?"

Tommy Morris grinned. "Come on, then, don't keep me in suspense! What tasty little morsel have you got lined up for me?"

A greasy palm waved towards the wall where the three half-naked women were back on their chairs. "I've brought three rent arrears cases along, not just one as there was last time. And you can, of course, have first choice."

The new arrival sauntered towards the three women and stared at each of them long and hard. The stocky one looked as if she might enjoy the experience, the older one had an air of resignation and the leggy one was unmistakably terrified.

"That's the one! Morris said, pointing at the latter. "You've done me proud!"

Tony Radford could sense genuine excitement in his associate's tone. "Glad to oblige! You can use the master bedroom."

Maisie grabbed the leggy girl by an arm, hauled her to her feet and led her towards the door to the hall and stairs. "You'd better co-operate to the full, or you'll be in big trouble!" she told the girl. "The master bedroom is second on the right," she told Morris.

Once Maisie had returned to the sitting room, her boss sidled up to her and asked if everything was in order.

"Yes, it should be all right, though it might be an idea to have the music back on," she whispered.

Radford nodded.

"OK, folks, let's get on with the party!" he told the gathering. "Come on, Lee, you haven't danced yet!"

Bob Wainwright, trousers at half-mast, downed yet another glass of claret before slumping into an armchair in a corner and gazing cross-eyed at the others, who, as far as he could discern, were all dancing.

Tony Radford, meanwhile, made sure that as soon as one piece of loud music stopped, another would start.

"I reckon you can have the older filly and Sam can have shorty," he said to Bains. "How does that suit?"

"That suits me fine," the developer replied. "She's no spring chicken, but, for all that, she's in pretty good shape!"

"Great! We've got a ground floor bedroom here. I'll show you where it is, and you can have a good time without disturbing our friend upstairs."

Maisie indicated where the room was.

"Where can I go?" wailed Sam.

"Don't be so bloody impatient! You can use the kitchen or the box room, but you can't go upstairs at the moment."

Maisie roared with laughter. "Don't burn your bum on a gas ring," she quipped with a grin.

The grin quickly turned into a grimace when she saw Tommy Morris reappear with bloodstains on various parts of his clothing.

"I have to go, and I'm afraid there's a bit of clearing up for you to do," he told Radford.

Morris was gone in a trice, and Radford rushed upstairs. On entering the master bedroom, he immediately called for Maisie.

"We've got another problem," he told her.

"Oh no, not again!"

"Yes, I'm afraid so. He's gone too far again, and this time it's pretty bad."

"Oh my God, it certainly is! We've got to get her to hospital straight away."

Radford wrapped a blanket round the young woman's inert form, and the pair carried the bundle downstairs and into Radford's car. Fortunately for him, the car was just a few feet from the front of the house and no one at the party or in the vicinity seemed to notice.

"The bedroom needs cleaning from top to bottom. You attend to that, and I will be back as soon as I can," he said.

The giant Addenbrooke's Hospital, on Cambridge's southern outskirts, was a two-mile drive away. The often-congested roads were comparatively clear, and Radford reached the roundabout that stood before the entrance within a few minutes.

Accident and Emergency was on the left, and Radford reasoned that the injured young woman would soon be seen if left just outside. He could then drive off without being seen himself and return to what was left of the party.

After finding Bob Wainwright slumped in an armchair as before, and noting, with relief, that the two couples were still where they had been before, he shot upstairs to the master bedroom. Maisie was on her hands and knees with a bowl of water, soap and a couple of dishcloths. A sheet, a pillowcase and two blankets all bloodstained, lay in a pile on the floor.

"There was blood all over the floor and walls, but I think I have managed to clear it all up," he was told.

"I guess the bedclothes will have to be incinerated. What a mess!"

"Yes, indeed!" the secretary agreed drily. "That Tommy Morris is a psycho, and we've been sailing a bit too close to the wind!"

Radford winced.

"How's the girl?" Maisie asked after a pause. "Everything happened so quickly that I'm not really sure what the extent of her injuries is."

"Blimey! I never thought of that! All I can say is thank God we've got her off our hands!"

About half an hour later, Tony Radford and his multi-tasking secretary were driving the other two rent defaulters home, with an assurance that their debts were now cleared. "Don't fall behind again!" they were warned.

Lee Bains was on his way back to Haverhill, feeling content and fulfilled.

Bob Wainwright, meanwhile, and with a bit of help, managed to recover from his state of drunken stupor. "Oh dear! Has everyone else gone home?" he enquired.

"Don't worry," his host assured him breathlessly. "The party turned out to be rather boring. You didn't miss anything!"

CHAPTER 9

A gentle squeeze of the hand made all the difference. When Frank regained consciousness, he found himself lying on a trolley that resembled a bed. There seemed to be constant comings and goings, and people everywhere.

"How are you feeling?" Laura asked with a beatific smile.

"All the better for seeing you," Frank replied. Such a response from anyone else, especially in different circumstances, might have appeared casual, even flippant. But here it was heartfelt, as the smile and the hand squeeze had conspired to nullify the dreaded trigger. Laura knew this, of course. Even now, she knew him like no one else could.

"You are in Accident and Emergency at Addenbrooke's," his former wife told him. "It's always busy here, I'm told, but a doctor will be checking you over to make sure you're fit to go home."

"Wherever that is!" Frank muttered.

"Don't worry about your tent and your bike," Laura said soothingly. "They're at our place, and you can claim them back when you're ready."

"How come?"

"Peter brought them back. He was the one who took you to hospital."

"How did he know where I was and what was happening?" As Frank became more alert, he became conscious of the pain in one side of his ribcage.

"Don't worry about that now," said Laura. "We can go into all that later, when you're feeling more up to it." Laura, who had had an uneasy feeling that Frank could be in hot water and had asked Peter to seek him out, smiled with a furrowed brow.

As Frank drifted into a half-sleep, a doctor appeared and examined him.

"You have a cracked rib and severe bruising, though, thankfully, it looks as if you have managed to protect your head," the doctor said. "You are going to need plenty of rest, and, for the next few days at least, someone will need to be around to keep an eye on you, in case your condition worsens… though that is unlikely."

Laura told the doctor a little about Frank's background and current lifestyle, and it was agreed that the best course was for Frank to camp in her back garden for the time being.

Frank thanked the doctor, though his biggest debts of gratitude were to be directed towards Laura and Peter, who had displaced him as the man in her life and yet was an ally rather than a foe. He mused over why a love rival would do anything to help him, let alone come to his rescue and, quite possibly, save his life.

He was even more thankful that another PTSD attack had been kept at bay.

Just before he left the forces, Frank had been urged by the powers that be to seek expert help in dealing with his condition. Frank had declined on the grounds that he could recognise the symptoms and had a strategy in place for tackling them. Another unstated reason was an inherent lack of trust, stemming from his childhood, in people charged with the job of looking after his wellbeing.

Perhaps he would seek help one day, anyway… but not now!

Frank was well aware that PTSD was far from rare among those who had experienced the horrors of war. He knew, too, that victims of other causes, such as sexual abuse including rape, civilian violence, psychological abuse and even people witnessing others suffering from trauma could be gripped by PTSD.

And Frank was well aware that flashbacks could come in various forms. They could be like a photograph, slide show or a video clip. They could feel almost as real as when the actual trauma originally occurred and be just as frightening.

He knew that flashbacks could take the form of words or phrases from the past. They could be accompanied by intense feelings of shame, sadness, and anger.

They could happen any time, anywhere, often without warning. They could be triggered by a time of year or day, by television programmes, films, smells, words, phrases, songs, places, someone serving a reminder of what had occurred in the past. They could be caused by pictures, tastes, fear, anxiety, and even sex.

They could occur straight away or sometime later.

Frank also knew that hearing voices telling him to do

things, such as harming himself or someone else, could be triggered. The voices were particularly terrifying, he found.

He had, however, worked out a coping mechanism, which, until now at any rate, he felt would suffice.

At the heart of this mechanism was control over thoughts and the need to think positively. Frank had compiled a list of things he should do. He kept this list with him at all times. And he frequently pulled it out of a buttoned-up pocket and referred to it. The list told him to:

- Be mentally detached whenever possible.
- Think about happy things when going to bed at night and when waking up in the morning.
- Start each day by telling himself how he wanted that day to be.
- Be as busy all day as possible, and not sit around thinking of his problems.
- Set a goal to achieve every day.
- Take regular exercise.
- Find reasons to laugh.
- Use positive words in conversation, and think positively.
- Visualise happy situations and events.

Frank had thought of adding; confiding in someone he could trust, but did not because of his inability to trust anyone – even Laura.

However, as he lay in his tent in Laura and Peter's garden later on, he was at least able to harbour happy memories.

His mind went back to the day when, as a twenty-year-old, he first met Laura at a barracks dance. The occasion marked the start of his first and only significant relationship. Up to that point, his experience with women had been limited to groping an orphanage matron, a few drunken snogs and a couple of visits to overseas brothels.

Frank was stationed at Aldershot at the time. A promising young soldier with a bright future predicted, he was destined to rise through the ranks and eventually earn a commission. At this stage, however, he was a mere lance-corporal.

News that a barracks dance was to be held was, as always, greeted with eager anticipation among the younger soldiers. As always, a band occupied a stage at one end of a large hall that usually served as a military lecture room. The officers and their wives sat at tables at the other end and the young men, on entering, stampeded towards a makeshift bar that occupied most of one of the walls. Frank and his comrades downed their pints while waiting for the coach that would carry the expected quota of local 'crumpet' that lived in the town or nearby villages.

A loud cheer went up as soon as a score or so women entered through one door and were directed by a waiting sergeant to the cloakroom they could use. There was another cheer when the women, aged between around twenty and forty, re-emerged and sat in a row on chairs opposite to the bar.

A few minutes later, Laura appeared, seemingly from nowhere, and went to sit with Major and Mrs Scanlon. Her slender but shapely figure and mane of black hair took Frank's breath away.

"It's not hard to guess what you're thinking!" the corporal sitting on the nearest stool said to him.

"You're quite right, and I'd be surprised if you're not thinking the same!" Having to come back to earth so abruptly after being bewitched made the retort a little testy.

The corporal grinned. "That's Laura Scanlon, and she figures in the dreams of half the blokes at Aldershot. Most of the other half are bent, so you can see she's quite something!"

Frank remained vaguely irritated. "All right, you cynical sod, how many of you get anywhere with her? Or do you just jerk off every night afterwards?"

The corporal's grin vanished. "Something tells me you've got it bad!" he said with a hint of seriousness. "Well, let me tell you that she's said to be unattainable. She's not seen that often at the barracks, anyway and when she is, all attempts to ask her out – never mind get round her– receive the brush-off."

"Straight up? Have there been many attempts?"

"Yes, quite a few, I'm told. She's not stuck-up or anything like that, and she always lets blokes down lightly, by all accounts. She might accept an invitation to dance, but that's all."

All Frank could think of saying was, "Good grief!"

The corporal grinned again. "Don't let anything I've said put you off, though. You might prove to be the exception. I wish you the best of luck!"

Frank watched the corporal walk towards the entrance end of the hall and disappear into the cloakroom reserved for men below the rank of lieutenant, before gazing towards the officers' table. The band had started playing and Laura was already busy bopping.

He stayed glued to his stool as a succession of potential suitors danced with Laura, talked to her for a minute or two and returned to wherever they had come from. Each face bore the hallmark of rejection.

Frank found the notion of being rebuffed unbearable, but the need to approach Laura outweighed such a fear. He got off his stool, waited for the music to stop and braced himself for action. As soon as the next dance was announced, he launched himself from the bar like a rocket and sped towards the officers' tables.

In so doing, he managed to beat another potential suitor by a yard and invited an involuntary "Ooh!" from Laura.

"Can I have this dance?" the two rivals blurted simultaneously.

"Thank you very much," Laura responded. "Well, you were first," she said to Frank before apologising to the rival.

Frank and Laura began a hesitant waltz.

"My name is Frank," the former said, aware that his palms were sweating.

"I'm Laura. Pleased to meet you." She looked even more beautiful than she did from a distance. Her eyes were a hypnotic black, her lips lightly rouged and her luxuriant black hair glowed under the half-dimmed lights. She wore a black, sleeveless dress with a high neckline and, although her figure was slender, her contours conspired to make Frank's knees weaken.

"I believe you're Major Scanlon's daughter."

"That's right. I live quite close by and I like to keep an

eye on my parents to make sure they're behaving!" The smile was magical.

Frank could feel the glow from Laura's eyes. He had never felt so gauche and nervous in his life, and he knew that she knew.

"Will you have another dance with me?" he ventured as soon as the music stopped.

"I'd love to," she replied, as black eyes gazed into blue.

The band stepped up the tempo and the pair parted and gyrated, one of them more gracefully than the other.

"Would you like to meet my parents?" Laura asked at the end. Without waiting for a reply, she took Frank's hand and led him to where the Scanlons were sitting.

Major Scanlon, who had been taking a keen interest in what had been going on, rose to his feet as they reached the table.

"You're Lance Corporal Pugsley, aren't you?" he said. "I have heard a lot of good things about you. Would you care to join us?"

As he lay inside his tent, Frank cherished the memory once more of his time at the table, when Major Scanlon and his wife chatted to him informally about military matters, current affairs and numerous other topics. Laura danced with him a few more times as well, and Frank became increasingly conscious of the warmth in the young woman's eyes.

Later, as the lights went low, Laura pressed herself against him as they danced and Frank had his first, fleeting taste of her lips.

The memory of the dance, and of subsequent events

that arose as the romance blossomed, often served to sustain him when a pulling of the PTSD trigger seemed imminent.

The next event in Frank's consciousness was dawn breaking. He put his head through the gap he had left at the front of his tent and saw Laura standing in the garden a few feet away.

"You slept well!" she said smiling. "It's almost ten o'clock!" The flecks of grey in her hair and the presence of a few worry lines had done nothing to diminish her desirability.

"Blimey, I'm sorry!"

"Don't worry," said Laura. "I'll bring out some breakfast for you in a few minutes, and you can have it in peace. How are you feeling now?"

"Much better, thanks." The pain in Frank's side was back, but it was not nearly so severe.

A moment later, Peter appeared.

"We've got three tickets for a Cambridge Crimewatch meeting, which starts in a couple of hours," he told Frank. "A friend who found he couldn't make it gave them to us. Because the weather's so good, it's going to be in someone's garden and you're welcome to come with us."

"Do come," Laura added. "The garden is at the house of one of Cambridge's richest businessmen and it's absolutely lovely, apparently."

"Why not. There's nothing like seeing how the other half lives!" Frank hoped, in hindsight, that his reply did not sound too caustic, as he felt more at peace with himself than he had for a long time.

Under the circumstances, it was just as well he had not heard about the drama that occurred while he lay on that trolley at Accident and Emergency. A half-naked, half-dead young woman, wrapped in a blanket, had been found outside and needed immediate treatment. The duty doctor was obliged to drop everything else to attend to her injuries, while a nurse made frantic telephone calls for back-up.

CHAPTER 10

ocktails, canapés, conversation at its most exquisite and a chance to admire landscaping that Capability Brown would have approved of were the order of the day at the annual Cambridge Crimewatch session.

The venue was in Porson Road, where the billionaire estate agent, auctioneer, racehorse owner and philanthropist had his Cambridge home.

Dominic Hawkins, whose collection of homes included properties in Newmarket, Chelsea, a remote part of the Cornish coast, Portugal and Florida, was arguably the wealthiest and most respected businessman in the region. His company, known simply as Hawkins, was the region's biggest and best known of its kind. The estate agency arm of Hawkins handled virtually all the region's top-of-the-market properties, as well as a good share of the others, that were put up for sale. The auctioneering side did so, too, and, in addition, dealt with everything from silverware and jewellery to farm machinery, and was often mentioned in the same breath as Sotheby's.

Dominic Hawkins himself was an ardent collector. Apart from a string of horses that regularly raced at

Newmarket and elsewhere, he was the owner of paintings by Rembrandt, Monet and Van Gogh, a range of Wedgwood vases and a collection of porcelain figurines.

His greatest pride and joy, though, was the range of gavels that he used with an undisguised passion whenever a deal was struck at one of his auctions. Some of the gavels were all wood, some were covered with steel, copper, brass or silver and one was gold-plated. Some bore intricate drawings or designs and all were well polished.

The gardens, clearly another source of pleasure for their owner, were being thrown open to ticket holders as an alternative to Trumpington Village Hall, the usual venue. Those attending the annual Cambridge Crimewatch meeting were given the opportunity to admire them before and after official business, and to sample the food and drinks on offer. The listed, eight-bedroom house was off limits, apart from a small section at one side, where cloakrooms could be accessed.

Frank felt obliged to don the best clothes he could muster, with Peter helping out with the loan of a blue blazer. Most of the hundred or so ticket holders had arrived by the time Laura, Peter and Frank filtered through the side entrance and walked onto a lawn that resembled a bowling green. To one side was a redundant marquee. To the other were tables laden with drinks and nibbles, and several of the Hawkins staff members were on hand to ensure that glasses and plates were not allowed to stay empty. In the middle were rows of chairs and a long mahogany table from which the presentation was to take place.

The ticket holders were standing and conversing in small groups, some expressing delight at the weather and at the setting they were in. A number were discussing the latest concerts due to be held in West Road or the performances to be enjoyed at the Arts Theatre.

While Laura and Peter were being greeted by a handful of people they knew, Frank's attention was diverted by a discussion amongst a well-heeled group of four on the subject of homelessness.

"They're not like the people starving in Africa or India," one member said. "People who are homeless in England are in that state because they choose to be."

"I'm not entirely convinced," another argued. "I think there's a lot more to it than that."

"I put it down to the Government's decision some years ago to close mental hospitals to save money and justifying that decision by calling it care in the community," a third member said. The fourth joined in with the observation that 'the tourists must find it quite an eyesore'.

Frank was entertaining the idea of offering the group his own views when his attention was diverted again, this time by the sight of a uniformed Steph Shawcross. He began to move towards her, but, as he did so, the sound of a bell and wood on wood could be heard.

"Please be seated," the ticket holders were invited by Dominic Hawkins.

The aristocratic auctioneer was at full volume, and, when the seats were on the verge of being all filled, he picked up each of the six gavels he had lined up in front of him and banged each of them down on the table twice. The audience had his full attention and, more importantly it seemed, was aware of the attachment he had to his gavels.

"Thank you for joining us for this, our sixth annual

Cambridge Crimewatch meeting, during which the aim is to offer expert advice, and to answer questions on the never-ending problem of preventing and tackling crime in our beloved city."

Dominic Hawkins was a tall, stately man in his mid-fifties with greying hair that showed no signs of thinning. He wore a sports jacket, flannels and an open-necked, checked shirt and, as always, exuded elegance and style.

"I would now like to hand you over once more to Inspector Bob Wainwright, who will offer you his words of wisdom and will be happy to answer questions and, on this occasion, is being assisted by WPC Stephanie Shawcross," he announced.

The burly Bob Wainwright had donned his best suit, a pinstripe, and a crisply pressed white shirt and rugby club tie for the occasion.

The main thrust of his short address was to emphasise the importance of home security.

"Burglaries are on the increase in Cambridge, especially in this particular locality, and we must all be increasingly vigilant," the inspector told his audience. He went on to describe the precautions householders could take and the various types of locks and alarms that were available.

"One useful step you can take is to photograph your most valuable items of jewellery, silverware and so forth," he advised.

Frank winced. "I'll photograph my crown jewels straight away," he whispered ironically.

Inspector Wainwright also recommended the setting up of Neighbourhood Watch schemes, before Steph

Shawcross gave a few tips on self-defence against muggers and demonstrated a few moves.

"Remember that the most important action is to do all you can not to get into such a situation in the first place," she emphasised.

Dominic Hawkins then rose to his feet, drew attention to a pile of crime prevention leaflets and invited questions.

Most of these related to home security, though one wag in the audience asked: "What would happen if someone went to an auction and made off with one of Mr Hawkins' gavels?"

The owner of the gavels roared with laughter and, before the police inspector could comment, he said: "That's way out of order! Let's just say that would be his lot!"

One of the group who had been talking about homelessness asked what one should do if accosted by a beggar.

"Do you mean an aggressive beggar?" the inspector asked.

"No. They can be, but aren't usually. What I really mean is should we give them money when one asks for some?"

Inspector Wainwright made a motion for WPC Shawcross to provide an answer.

"No," she said. "The money will almost certainly be spent on drugs or drink. We need to look at other ways we can help homeless people, many of whom have mental health issues."

"Giving them money perpetuates the problem," the inspector said, cutting in. "It's also worth bearing in mind that a lot of the beggars you see on the street are not really homeless at all, but conmen who see begging as an easy way to make a living."

Another member of the audience asked: "Are drugs behind a lot of the problems in Cambridge?"

"Yes, they are," the inspector answered tersely. "It's a growing problem, and we are doing our utmost to stamp it out. A lot of crime is, of course, fuelled by addicts seeking cash to pay for their habit. We have a leaflet on the subject, and you're welcome to study it. Next question!"

The next question related to what sort of valuables should be photographed and what were the best types of camera to use. Inspector Wainwright smiled expansively, repeated what he had said earlier and recommended the city's most prestigious photographic shop.

The presentation ended on a humorous note, when a muscular audience member asked WPC Shawcross to demonstrate her self-defence skills once more. When she invited him to come forward and try to grab her, she put him in a hammerlock from which he could not escape.

An amused Hawkins banged on the table with each of his six gavels and suggested bringing official business to a close.

"For the next hour, you are all welcome to enjoy your drinks and nibbles, wander round the gardens and, of course, help yourselves to one of the crime prevention leaflets we have provided."

While Laura and Peter chatted to the handful of people they knew, Frank explored the gardens and found them to be unexpectedly extensive. Hidden behind the hedgerows were more lawns, all well manicured, along with picture postcard flowerbeds, fountains, shrubs, rows of trees and, at the furthermost point from the house, a stream and a small cottage. Frank guessed that the latter was home for a resident gardener.

The stream, which was connected to a pond with a fountain at one end, bubbled gently as it made its way beneath the wire fence that acted as the property's rear boundary. Frank fancied he saw a water vole swimming hurriedly away from him as he approached. He spotted a nest on the opposite bank and gazed at a small shoal of fish just inches from his feet.

"To him that has shall be given," he said aloud.

"It's an unfair world!" a woman's voice announced. Frank turned round to see Steph Shawcross standing a few feet away. "I understand you've been looking for me."

Frank quickly regained his composure. "Absolutely. I thought we could have a spot of lunch together."

"I'm flattered, though I suspect that it's not just for the pleasure of my company," Steph said.

"Your company's always a pleasure, Steph. I hope it's all right for me to call you that, though, as you know, I am on the lookout for information."

"OK, but it's probably best if we don't talk too much here. My boss will wonder where I have got to if I'm away for too long."

"Fair enough. How about a bite at the Fort, then?"

"That's fine. One thing I can tell you here and now, though, is that the man found dead in the Cam was that Fretwell fellow. Everyone knew him as Toby, I believe."

"Right!"

"Right! You don't look surprised and I'm not surprised that you're not surprised!"

"I wonder if you could do me a favour," Frank asked as he prepared to depart with Laura and Peter. "I would like to look up some friends in Mill Road. There are plenty of buses, so there should be no difficulty in getting back to you afterwards."

"No problem," said Peter. "We can go there right now."

About a quarter of an hour later, Frank was making his way towards the van where Adrian and Germaine lived. The part of Mill Road that he walked along seemed to be unusually seedy. Four meths drinkers had taken over a bus shelter and their smells travelled almost as far as their oaths. Rough sleepers were occupying more doorways than ever, one unkempt man was lurching along the middle of the road, and the pavements were strewn with cigarette ends, the remnants of takeaway meals and their wrappings, and a couple of abandoned needles.

The area around the van was, if anything, worse. Adrian and Germaine were busy clearing up dog excrement.

"What's the coffee situation?" Frank asked as he arrived.

"The coffee situation is good, if nothing else!" said Germaine.

"How are things?" Adrian asked as the three friends sipped their brews.

Frank described the beating he had received from the bikers. "How about you? You don't look any too happy?"

"We're not and we're not quite sure what's going on," said Germaine. "We're getting more and more dogs coming here and making their messes. But that's not all, something isn't right."

"How do you mean?"

"It might be just our imagination, but we feel we are being watched," said Adrian. "We often see a big bloke with a bomber jacket and close-cropped hair hanging around, and we get the impression he's spying on us."

"It's really creepy," Germaine added. "I'm now frightened of being left on my own."

CHAPTER 11

"**Y**ou talk too much!" said Kirk.

"No, I don't, I just try to be sociable," Billy Newton replied. "Surely it's better to be chatty than down in the dumps and not talking at all!"

"That depends," said Liam.

"On what?"

"You need to use your loaf," Kirk said, as he finished his coffee, picked up his pile of *Big Issues* and left Overstream House, the building occupied by the homelessness charity Wintercomfort.

Billy had heard about the attack on Frank and was holding forth about the 'X Factor', their likely involvement and what they got up to generally.

"You should know by now that shooting your mouth off can get you into big trouble," Liam said. "Walls have ears, you know."

"What, even the walls of Wintercomfort?"

"That's exactly what I mean. You shouldn't trust anybody." Liam gave a sidelong glance towards the diminutive Phil, a regular user of the services provided by Wintercomfort and known among some as 'The Weasel'.

The Wintercomfort services included providing breakfasts and lunches, laying on legal advice and offering a certain amount of vocational training. The number of users receiving meals at Overstream House had risen from around twenty to forty or more in the space of two years. The number of rough sleepers had, without doubt, risen inexorably, too, and the same probably applied to Cambridge's hidden homeless – the people who slept on friends' floors or in temporary accommodation.

Big Issue sellers would pop in and collect their weekly quota of copies of the magazine, and were allowed to pocket half of the sale proceeds.

"Those X Factor blokes are dangerous, and it's not sensible to upset them," Liam added.

"OK, I take your point, though I'd love to see this guy Pugsley sort out Morris and those other jokers!"

With that, Billy picked up his bundle of *Big Issues* and headed for the exit. "See you later, folks. Keep smiling and never stop begging!" he quipped.

"Kirk's right," Phil muttered. You're too mouthy for your own good!"

Billy, who was already later than usual, descended the stone steps close to Overstream House that provided quick access to Midsummer Common and strolled along the side of the River Cam for a while, before turning right and traversing the grass and heading towards King Street and his city centre sales patch.

Before leaving the river, he passed the Fort St George, where Frank and Steph were seated at an outside table and sipping red wine.

Frank called out: "Hi Billy! How are things?" The

words fell on deaf ears, however, as the fantasy-driven former drug addict dreamed of conquering the world with his charm and bringing an end to Tommy Morris's tyranny.

"You seem to know the local down-and-outs better than we do," Steph observed. She was now out of uniform and looking fit and relaxed in a T-shirt and jeans.

"Could be," Frank agreed. "The lifestyle I lead brings me into contact with a lot of people, who, for the want of a better word, society don't notice or, at any rate, choose not to notice."

"Point taken, though believe me, there are quite a few of society's outcasts the police take more than a passing interest in."

"What about Tommy Morris or Tony Radford?"

Steph sighed. "Their names are known to us, especially Morris's. I have been studying a few files since I first met you, and seen that Morris first came on our radar fifteen years ago as a juvenile delinquent accused of GBH. It transpired that he had been terrorising a neighbourhood for two or three years before that, and he was sent to a detention centre. They found him impossible to handle there, and the next step was to have him sectioned under the Mental Health Act."

"So he's something of a psycho then! What happened next?"

Steph placed a hand on one of his hands for a moment. "Nothing," she said. "He remained sectioned for six months and, since then, he joined a martial arts club and is now one of its stars."

"But what about all this talk of him being a feared drugs dealer and the head of a gang of local heavies?"

Steph touched Frank's hand again and pressed it. "All hearsay, I'm afraid. There has been lots of talk, but no proof."

"What does your boss Wainwright, or whatever his name is, have to say about it?"

Steph's face reddened for a moment, and Frank sensed that relations with her boss left a lot to be desired. "Very little, I'm afraid," she said eventually. "When I do talk about Morris or Radford, for that matter, he either clams up, changes the subject or assigns me to a tedious task he wants done straight away."

"It sounds as if he's giving you a bad time; is he harassing you as well, by any chance?"

Steph went red again, and she gave Frank a pat on the leg. "You also wanted to know about Radford. The only thing we've got on him is that he was once questioned on suspicion of tax evasion, but nothing came of it. There has also been talk of him charging extortionate rents and having tenants intimidated into either paying these rents or quitting their homes."

Frank and Steph sipped their wine and sat in silence for a while as a passing punt and a fleeing moorhen took their attention.

Frank sensed that Steph was holding something back. He gazed at her buttercup blonde hair that had been allowed to drop onto her shoulders and at a pair of pale blue eyes that exuded brightness, determination, strength and vulnerability at the same time.

"You might not believe it, but I have been known to be discreet in my time." His tone was as reassuring as he could manage.

Steph placed her right hand on Frank's left thigh and gave it a squeeze. "You're quite right, there is something else I can tell you, though I hope to God you're as discreet as you say you are."

"I'm all ears!" said Frank, who somehow managed to stay poker-faced.

Steph put her head in her hands, before telling Frank that 'a massive drugs overdose' was almost certainly the cause of Toby's death. "It has still to go before the coroner, but everything I have heard points to that."

Sensing that there was still more to come, Frank suggested there was "quite a lot you might have heard".

"Are you sure you can be discreet?" Steph pleaded, a hand descending on Frank's leg once more. "What I have to tell you could get me into real trouble!"

"Yes, yes, for God's sake, yes!" Frank was no longer able to conceal his emotions. "You know what I want. I want to find out what really happened to my son. I'm not satisfied with the official story, and anything you can tell me will be received with the utmost gratitude and discretion." He removed the hand resting on his leg and squeezed it gently.

Steph took a deep breath. "All right, here goes! The first thing I know is that my boss, Inspector Wainwright frequently meets Tony Radford for drinks at the Fountain. He often comes back from the pub reeking of alcohol."

"Does that mean the pair are in cahoots in some way?"

"Yes, I believe it does. I can't prove anything, of course, but I've also heard Wainwright talking to Radford on the phone. A lot of the time, they're just exchanging the latest blue jokes they've heard, but I've also heard conversations about how Radford managed to get away with charging exorbitant rents on his properties. One conversation was about how Radford managed to get a woman of ninety to quit her home by having a hole dug in front if it so that a developer could move in and take over."

"What were Wainwright's reactions?"

"Oh, he treated it all as a huge joke," said Steph. "And I once heard Wainwright use the phrase, 'That's the sort of percentage I would be a fool to turn down.'"

"Strewth! Now I've heard everything!"

"No, you haven't! Not quite, anyway! In one conversation between Wainwright and Radford, the name Pugsley came up I don't mean you, I mean your son."

Frank's pulse was at full throttle. "Go on!"

"Mention was made of your Terry getting a job at the John Smith Stables in Newmarket. It was brought up shortly after his death, and I didn't hear anything else."

"OK, so who's the boss at the John Smith Stables?"

"They're owned by Dominic Hawkins, the same Dominic Hawkins who presided over the Cambridge Crimewatch meeting. I gather he gave the stables that name to make it sound quintessentially English, and flew in the face of the growing Arab influence on the Newmarket horseracing industry."

Frank made no attempt to hide his excitement. "I'm really grateful for what you've just told me. You've given me quite a bit to go on. And rest assured, I will be discreet and do nothing to put your position in jeopardy."

A tear fell onto the table close to Steph's half-empty glass. "I hope I have been a bit of help, but I have a feeling I won't be able to help anymore in the future."

Frank felt asking 'why' was unnecessary.

"That man Wainwright is a fat slob and a bastard!" he was told. "He was making suggestive remarks within a week of me starting work at Parkside and when I spurned his advances he got nasty. He has been criticising my work at every opportunity recently and giving me every unpleasant task he can think of."

"Is there anywhere else at Parkside where you can work and be away from him?"

"That's a possibility I'm considering asking for, though I think Wainwright is trying to get me transferred to another nick altogether. One reason, I suspect, is that he's recently been aware that I overheard some of his conversations and he wants me out of the way."

"I'm really sorry," said Frank. "I wish there was something I could do to help you."

Steph took one of Frank's hands with both of hers and held it for a moment. "Don't worry. I will get through this somehow. I have enjoyed knowing you and hope we can remain in touch."

Without further ado, she rose from her chair and half-sauntered, half-jogged towards the city centre.

Frank sat, sipped the last of his wine and mused for a while. His meeting with Steph had brought forth such an amalgam of thoughts that he needed to settle for a while to enable him to decide which one to address first. He gave his sore side a rub and found solace in the knowledge that his recuperative powers were well above average.

In the end, he decided to head for the city centre himself to seek out Billy on the off-chance that the loquacious *Big Issue* seller could expand on what Steph had said, especially about finding employment at stables in Newmarket.

Just before reaching Boots, however, he remembered that there was a Hawkins office almost exactly opposite and decided to try to get an audience with the proprietor.

On entering, he could see immediately that the whole place dripped with wealth. Chairs, tables, desks, carpeting and walls with wood panelling all bore the hallmark of tasteful opulence. Six well-heeled members of staff were busy behind computers or handling telephone calls.

Frank approached the reception area, where he was greeted by a young woman with the figure of a model and a face that would not be out of place in *Country Life*.

"You're in luck," the smiling receptionist said. "Mr Hawkins will be going out shortly, but he can see you for five minutes." She led Frank to an oak door and knocked.

Dominic Hawkins' office was the most impressive and tasteful Frank had ever seen. Its floor area almost matched that of an average-sized house. Its carpet was superior even to the one in the reception area. There were polished mahogany tables and chairs, leather armchairs, paintings and photographs on the walls and two shelves containing a collection of silver trophies including a replica of a racehorse. In addition, a bookcase laden with a range of classical literature, as well as manuals devoted to horseracing, collecting, auctioneering and estate agency.

Dominic Hawkins was seated behind a massive black desk. Frank could not fail to notice that, apart from a sophisticated computer, a telephone and trays carrying paperwork, the collection of gavels he had seen at the Crimewatch meeting had been laid out in a line.

"Do come in and take a seat," the smiling proprietor said. Frank took the one closest to the desk. Hawkins offered him a cigar and, after Frank declined, said: "I hope you won't mind if I do."

After selecting one of the smaller ones from a pinewood box, he reached for the gavel that lay furthest to his left and pressed a button to one side to make a flame appear.

"You might have heard that my collection of auctioneers' gavels is as much a pride and joy to me as my racehorses," he beamed. "And, as you can see, they can be customised to do more than just close a sale."

"Very impressive," Frank agreed.

"Anyway, please excuse me for wittering on. I'm sure you're not here to admire my objets d'art. How can I help you?"

Frank faltered for a moment as he mentally compared Dominic Hawkins' appearance with his own. He had donned the best clothes he could muster, but these hardly matched his host's Savile Row suit, which had been cut to fit like a glove. Fortunately there was not even a hint of disapproval from the elegant Mr Hawkins.

"I will be glad to help if I can."

Frank's explanation of why he was in Cambridge was greeted with sympathetic noises.

"That sounds absolutely terrible," said Hawkins. "I'm truly sorry to hear of your loss, and if there's any way I can help I will gladly do so."

"Well, I've heard on the grapevine that Terry worked for you for a while at your stables in Newmarket. Is that true?"

Dominic Hawkins strummed the top of his desk for a moment before picking up his telephone. "Could you bring in the John Smith Stables folder, please?" he was heard to say.

"The name rings no bells, but there might be something on file," he told Frank. "We take on quite a few people short term, some of them on work experience. There are lots of comings and goings, and I must confess that I am not familiar with every name."

A young woman brought in a folder, and her boss thumbed through it. "Sorry, there's nothing here. Perhaps you could give me some contact details, in case something comes to light later on. I'm not expecting it to, to be honest, but you never know."

CHAPTER 12

Buskers of all kinds could be seen vying for attention by the time Frank walked out of the Hawkins office.

At the junction of St Andrew's Street and Market Street a bearded young man was playing a violin while standing on the loosest of tightropes. Another young man with just the beginning of a beard was spinning inside a giant hoop near the entrance to Petty Cury. Three trumpeters were demonstrating their expertise in front of the Guildhall, and there was a variety of singers – some melodic, some tuneless. A thin old man with a weather-beaten face was chanting something indiscernible while tapping a piece of metal with a spoon. His presence was a regular feature of the city centre, as was the wizened old woman's cello strumming, which was virtually drowned out by the hubbub created by tourists.

The tourists were, of course, a regular source of income for buskers and, to some extent, the *Big Issue* sellers. There were times when the absence of visitors from the United States meant every tongue bar English could be heard in and around the Market Square. The pushy punt touts had been moved on, though now and again there were people lurking in Petty Cury and seeking funds to help charities or the less than charitable. Frank could not help wondering why the opening sales gambit was nearly always, "How are you today?" when what they really meant was, "How big is your wallet?"

Billy Newton was standing outside Boots as usual. His sales patter, inviting passers-by to "join the shortest queue in Cambridge" was being delivered with his customary charm and good humour and, despite the competition for attention, he had managed to secure three sales. The profusion of passers-by meant he did not see Frank until he was within touching distance. His feelings about Frank were ambivalent, though on this occasion, the thought that he could cause trouble for Tommy Morris and his gang transcended fears for his own safety.

"Hi there, Frank! Great to see you!" he said, while warmly shaking his hand. "You look as if you're on the mend."

Frank, by now well aware of Billy's ability to keep his ear to the ground, confirmed that he was feeling much better.

"Is there any way I can help you?" Billy asked.

"There might be. I've heard on the grapevine that my son Terry worked at the John Smith Stables in Newmarket for a while. Do you know anything about that?"

Billy, looking thoughtful for a moment, replied: "Can't say that I do. Sorry."

"Do you know anyone who might know? I'm probably clutching at straws here, but if you don't know I fear no one will."

Billy rubbed his chin and pondered the question, and then suddenly his face lit up. "Yes, I've just remembered that I've met one of the stable lads working there. I've only met him once and don't really know him, and I'm not even sure if he's still there. But when I met him, he said he'd worked at John Smith's for several years. So if your Terry was there at the time, he would surely have known him."

"Do you have a name?"

"Er, yes, it's Ernie Foster, or Fossey, or something like that. The Christian name is Ernie, anyway."

"That's great!" said Frank. "I will make a point of going to Newmarket and seeing him."

"Good luck!" There was now vehemence in Billy's tone. "I have a feeling this Ernie fella is none too bright and he certainly doesn't speak very well, but, assuming you find him, you should at least get to know if Terry worked at those stables."

"I will do my damnedest!"

"Tell you what, I could come with you and make the introduction. There's nothing that would give me more pleasure than seeing Morris get his comeuppance. He's ruined a lot of lives, and, more and more, his victims seem to be teenagers like your Terry and I would really love to see him rot in hell!"

"Great!" said Frank. "Why don't we meet right here at 9am tomorrow?"

"Why not? It will cost me a few sales, but it will be worth it."

Frank decided to look up Adrian and Germaine again. He had an uneasy feeling they were being targeted because of their association with him, and felt duty-bound to advise them to move to a different part of Cambridge or even quit the city altogether.

On arrival, his worst fears were confirmed. The stench of dog excrement surrounding their van was almost unbearable. As Frank weaved his way through the piles of excrement plus needles, cigarette ends and other rubbish, he saw Germaine feverishly applying a damp cloth to one side of the van. He then saw the words, in block capitals, 'SILENCE IS GOLDEN' had been sprayed on with gold paint. Each letter was about a foot high.

Germaine saw Frank and turned to greet him, and Frank could see she had a black eye.

"We're getting out of here," she said, half-sobbing. "Adrian's taken quite a battering and he's having a lie-down. It's just as well you turned up when you did because in another hour, we'll be gone."

"I'm really sorry. Where will you go?"

"As far away as possible," an emerging Adrian told him with a ruefully lopsided smile. Frank noticed that, apart from a swollen face, he was having difficulty moving.

"That's probably the best thing you can do, though it's hardly what I want. I'm almost certain you were set upon because of your association with me."

"Perhaps you should get out of Cambridge, too," said Germaine. "The three thugs who attacked us were as nasty as they come, and you are clearly in danger yourself. You're playing with fire and we both fear for your safety."

"Leaving Cambridge is not an option for me," Frank replied. "You know it isn't. The more I think about how my son died, the more I feel the whole situation smells."

"We expected you to say something like that," said Adrian. "In many ways, I wish I could stay and stand shoulder to shoulder with you while your investigations continue. But, to be honest, I don't have the stomach for it any more, and am probably no longer up to it either."

Frank patted him gently on the shoulder. "Don't worry. You're a good friend, you both are, and I hope we will continue to stay in touch."

"You can count on it," Germaine promised. "We go back a long way, and nothing changes that."

Billy Newton, meanwhile, was on his way back to the hostel he shared with Kirk, Lee and Phil, among others, in Milton Road, a stone's throw from Overstream House. Despite his late start that day, he had managed to secure more sales than usual and was in an upbeat mood.

As he turned into Milton Road from Chesterton Road, there was a sudden shower from a darkening cloud. As a consequence, he failed to see the formidable form in front of him until he had almost collided with it.

"You just don't listen, do you?" the stocky, balaclava-wearing man barring his way said. "You just won't learn to keep your mouth shut, will you?"

"I don't know what you're talking about?" Billy replied.

The man in front of him was known as Einstein. He was Tommy Morris's Number Two and reputed to be the brains behind the power of the X Factor. Although only 5ft 7ins tall and less outwardly wild in demeanour than Morris, he was immensely strong and capable of being just as vicious.

"Yes, you do. You've been running your mouth again!"

"In what way?" Billy was desperately trying to think on his feet.

"You know perfectly well what. You're beginning to bore me!"

Einstein administered a backhand slap that had Billy reeling against a hedgerow.

"You might call this a meeting of the minds," Einstein said with a smirk. "Newton, the expert on gravity, meets Einstein, the relativity expert!"

Billy was uncharacteristically mute for a moment.

"I'm hoping that, by now, you're appreciating the GRAVITY of the situation you're in! And, by the time I have finished with you, someone will need to contact your RELATIVES!" Einstein was looking increasingly smug.

"You have quite a sense of humour!"

"Thank you," Einstein said as he delivered another slap, making Billy bleed inside his mouth.

"Where's your boss?" Billy asked, as he tried to think of ways to get out of his predicament.

"He's out of town and left me in charge. Why, do you think I'm not running things the way he thinks I should?" Einstein felled Billy with a right-hand punch and kicked him in the stomach. He ordered him to get up. "I haven't finished giving you your lesson on gravity yet!" he snarled.

Billy slowly got onto his hands and knees. As he did so, he saw a pile of loose chippings in loose soil on the pavement and, next to them, a wooden plank. The rain was beginning to fall harder, making the pavement slippery and vision slightly blurred.

"I said, get up!" Einstein ordered again.

Billy rose slowly to his feet and, without warning

hurled a handful of chippings and soil into Einstein's eyes. As his tormentor reeled backwards in pain, he brought the plank down onto his head as hard as he could. Einstein's knees buckled and Billy delivered blow after blow with the plank until the X Factor's feared Number Two was lying inertly in a pool of blood.

At first, he did not know where to flee. All he knew was that he dare not go back to the hostel and had to get out of Cambridge as soon as he could. After a couple of hundred yards, he stopped to collect his thoughts. He realised he was heading for the Chesterton Fen area and a possible short-term refuge.

The pain from the beating he had received was beginning to sink in, and Billy was obliged to stagger rather than run to where Jack, a former *Big Issue* seller and fellow Wintercomfort user, was currently living. Every one of the last 300 yards to the terraced house he sought brought hurt. Eventually he reached two wooden posts, which once had a gate between them, and a postage stamp lawn with almost as many nettles and thistles as blades of grass.

The front door was devoid of a bell or knocker. Its handle was loose, and just a few flakes of green paint remained on its wood. Billy's first knock went unanswered, so he banged and banged again until footsteps could be heard coming downstairs. A skinny girl of about twenty and wearing nothing but a towel and the glazed look of a drug addict appeared.

"Is Jack in?" Billy asked before collapsing.

A couple of miles away, Laura was on her way home from a shopping trip. She had taken a bus to the city centre, having made the decisions to augment what lay in the larder and to give the car a rest. She had bought eggs, bread, soup, rolls and a variety of fruit and vegetables.

The expedition had been uneventful, save an uneasy feeling she was being watched. The unease increased when a rough-looking young man with tattooed biceps bulging from beneath a T-shirt bounded onto the bus home just seconds before the journey got under way.

The walk from the bus stop where Laura got off was just a short one, and she moved as briskly as her bags of goods permitted. She was no more than 100 yards from home when the young man caught her up and barred her way.

"Would you like me to carry your bags?" he asked.

Laura responded with a polite "No, thank you."

The young man stepped aside and then caught up with her again. "You're a friend of Frank Pugsley, aren't you?"

"Yes, I am. What's it to you?" Laura responded curtly.

The next thing she knew was one of her bags being knocked out of her hand and its contents spilled onto the pavement. The eggs were cracked and a paving stone became yellow with the yolk.

"Oh dear!" the young man said with a smirk. "That's the trouble with eggs they're so easily broken!"

CHAPTER 13

A pungent cocktail of smells greeted Billy when he opened his eyes and found himself lying on a lumpy mattress next to a wall in a smoke-filled room. The room was dimly lit and effectively half dark. Eyes from all angles were focused on him. The eyes bore no hint of curiosity, just resignation. The room, although not exceptionally large, extended the length of the house. The foot of an exposed staircase was less than a yard from where Billy gained admission, and to one side of the room was a tiny recess with space for a sink and a gas ring.

"Jack's not around," said a voice from somewhere.

"You're Billy Newton, the *Big Issue* seller, aren't you?" another voice asked.

Billy found he was able to sit up almost painlessly. He could see what looked like a reefer being passed round. "Yes, that's me. Will Jack be back?" He could now see six young men and two girls… at least he thought they were girls… sitting in a half-circle.

"Don't know, sorry," said the first voice. "I think he owes someone some money and he's lying low for a while."

"Which means he might be back, might not," someone else volunteered.

"Are you in trouble yourself?" one of the girls asked.

"I need somewhere to crash for a night, and then I'm going to have to disappear for a spell."

"You're welcome to crash here," said the man who knew who he was. There was not a shred of surprise from anyone about Billy's predicament.

"I reckon you and I have something in common," a long-haired youth, sitting on his own in a corner, said.

The youth, thin, gaunt and looking no more than fifteen, described how he had been to an illegal rave in the village of Milton, three miles to the north of Cambridge, when the police raided.

"They burst in with their batons, belting everyone they could get close to," he said. "I just ran for it, leaving my best leather coat behind. There were loads of police cars outside, but it was dark and no one saw me get away. I had got there in a friend's car and I don't know what happened to him. My parents think I'm at home in bed. We live at Sawston and they'll go mad when they find I'm not at home!"

"Well, at least you escaped a battering!" another youth, who looked only slightly older, interjected. "I've got that bastard Bainbridge on my back!"

"And if you've any sense, you'll pay him quickly," the girl wearing a towel said. "Bainbridge works for Tommy Morris, and you know what he's like!"

"That reminds me, how's Ellie now?" one of the other girls asked.

"She's alive, but that's all you can say! She's out of

hospital, but still in a bad way. She's too terrified to talk to the fuzz, of course. So Morris gets away with it once more!"

"And Radford keeps his nose clean, too," a bearded young man holding a pipe and a cigarette lighter added.

At this point, the sound of a door shutting made the group look upwards to see a powerfully built but overweight man zipping up his trousers and walking heavily down the bare wooden stairs. He gave the girl with the towel a wink and departed through the front door.

The object of his attention said: "That's this month's rent sorted, anyway!"

"Was that who I thought it was?" Billy asked.

"I'm afraid so," said the man with the beard. "Radford's got it all sewn up. He's loaded with money and even has a copper in his pocket!"

The copper in question had begun to become a cause for concern, in fact. Heavy drinking and increasingly erratic behaviour were serving as warning signals that Bob Wainwright's powers of discretion might not be what they were.

Tony Radford mused over the matter while sitting in an upstairs room above his city centre estate agency office. It was first thing in the morning, and his staff were yet to arrive. He had a radio on because he found the airwaves, in some mysterious way, were often able to help him marshal his thoughts as well as keep up to date with the news.

Currently on the air were the Chief Secretary to the Treasury and two national newspaper journalists. The topic for discussion was Britain's economy, and the Minister was announcing that exports were up and unemployment down, and that there was every chance that Britain's trade deficit would be reduced significantly.

Radford, who was sitting by a window, leaned downwards to see a group of beggars congregating on a street corner, two rough sleepers lying in bundles in doorways, a syringe on a pavement and a menacing-looking young man in punk attire who appeared to be conducting a drugs transaction. The irony of a sight that flew in the face of the broadcast was not lost on him. But there were more pressing matters to consider.

One of these was the behaviour of Bob Wainwright. Having a 'tame copper' in tow had been extremely useful at times. However, if he was starting to become a loose cannon, he could become a liability. So he needed to be kept an eye on.

Tommy Morris might need to be watched, too. His conduct at the party in Hopper Street had been way over the top, but at least he had had the sense to disappear for a while until any potential hullabaloo was over. Apart from that, Einstein was always on hand to smooth things over if necessary.

Meanwhile, Radford also had cause to look on the bright side. Rents had continued to swell the coffers, and it was always possible to secure some sort of 'payment in kind' arrangement if a tenant could not come up with the cash.

The icing on the cake, though, was the latest deal he had struck with the Haverhill-based developer, Lee Bains. It involved demolishing a small block of run-down flats, developing the land, building a new, up-market block and eventually selling the entire site at a massive profit. Land values had been soaring, and Messrs Radford and Bains could not lose!

The one obstacle, in the form of a family who could not be persuaded to move, had been cleared. On returning from a holiday on the coast, they found themselves mysteriously without a bathroom, WC or back door. Rats were running amok, too. There were no neighbours left to talk to and the landlord Radford always seemed to be out.

The family was now gone, and Radford was confident that he could handle any form of comeback.

He looked out of the window again and saw that the down-and-outs were still there. Not his problem!

It was a matter for a man born with a silver spoon in his mouth, the snooty Dominic Hawkins, to deal with!

Perhaps it was pure coincidence that, at that very moment, the aristocratic auctioneer Hawkins was looking at how he could get support for the 'Wake up with Wintercomfort' initiative. He was determined to demonstrate that he had a community spirit.

A year ago, he had thrown his weight behind a refurbishment project at Jimmy's Night Shelter in East Road. The shelter had been named after the late Jim Dilley, who had spent much time sleeping rough in the region and, towards the end, had made his home under an M11 motorway bridge. The shelter had previously offered accommodation in crammed dormitories. Now there were around twenty self-contained units with beds, wardrobes, sinks, showers and WCs.

The previous year, he had helped Britain's first

Emmaus community at Landbeach, a few miles to the north of Cambridge, by providing a vanload of second-hand furniture, some of which could be restored and sold on. The people living in the community were known as 'companions' and carried out various kinds of work to earn their keep. Many were able to move on to paid jobs and their own homes later on.

The Cambridge Foodbank had received his support, too.

The current project entailed encouraging members of the public to invite friends and neighbours round for breakfast at a small price and passing on the proceeds to Wintercomfort. Much of the idea was, of course, to raise awareness of the growing problem of homelessness.

Dominic Hawkins pored through a file marked 'Local Charities' that lay on his monolith of a desk, and pondered the question of how his help could be most effective.

As he did so, a sudden commotion could be heard from the reception area. A fist was banging on a desk, chairs were being thrown around and there was a string of expletives. Heavy footsteps approached a door, which was thrown open, before the door to Dominic Hawkins' private office swung open and a mountain of a man lurched into the room. He was 6ft 6in tall and must have weighed at least twenty stone.

"I want my money!" the man bellowed, as he staggered towards Dominic Hawkins' desk. The alcohol in his breath became increasingly apparent with each unsteady step.

"What makes you think I owe you money?" he was asked. "I don't even know who you are."

"The name's O'Reilly, Rick O'Reilly and I want my money!"

The aristocratic auctioneer already knew him to be the notorious bar room brawler and a bane in the lives of the local police. His face had appeared in the local press, and the story of his encounter with Frank Pugsley had reached him, too.

He was a man who liked to be informed about anything and everything. He guessed, correctly, that O'Reilly, in his inebriated state, had entered the wrong premises.

"Are you sure you're in the right place?" he asked coolly. "This is an estate agents and auctioneers' office."

O'Reilly realised his mistake instantly. He had been due to meet someone he had lent money to in a supermarket-cum-café fifty yards away. But he did not want to admit his mistake.

"Are you trying to be funny?" he bellowed. A massive fist landed on a monolithic desk.

The man behind the desk remained cool. But, although he held no fears for his own safety, the risk of damage to his property, caused him concern.

He eyed his orderly line of gavels and picked up an elegant implement that was encased in copper plating.

"Give me my money!" O'Reilly roared. "If you know what's good for you, you'll do it now!"

Dominic Hawkins pointed one end of the copper-plated gavel towards his antagonist and pressed a button at the other end.

Rick O'Reilly flew backwards and fell onto the floor clutching his chest. As he did so, the office door opened and a terrified receptionist ushered in the firm's two security men.

"Are you all right, sir?" one of the men asked.

"No problem!" his boss assured him. "The poor fellow's had a bit too much of the sauce and blundered into my office by mistake. Make sure he's all right before you see him off the premises, please."

After the men had gone, the receptionist continued to stay rooted to the spot, gaping. She received reassurance, too, when, gleefully told: "I always wanted to know how effective plastic bullets could be. Now I do, they worked a treat!"

The receptionist continued to stand open-mouthed for a moment longer, before asking: "I hope I was right to call our security men and not the police?"

"What you did was fine," she was told. "The poor fellow was off his face with booze. He's a troubled soul who didn't know what he was doing. He's not likely to come back, and I feel no need to add to his troubles by involving the police."

Rick O'Reilly half-walked, half-stumbled towards the pubs of King Street before remembering that they had all barred him. So he continued to head northwards towards the river, in the general direction of home. As he walked towards the Elizabeth Way bridge, Riverside and Stourbridge Common, he almost collided with Frank Pugsley, who was heading in the opposite direction. O'Reilly lurched blindly onwards, oblivious to the other man's sardonic smile.

A few minutes later, Frank was under the bridge. He had heard that there were once plans to erect a night shelter for the homeless underneath it. However, people living nearby had objected and, among other things, pointed out that a primary school was just a few hundred yards away, and the plans were shelved. The pavement looked clean, save the presence of one abandoned needle, and there were no unkempt down-and-outs around to sully the scenery. Or so it initially appeared…

Behind a pillar in a corner could be heard the unmistakable sound of a beating being administered. On investigating, Frank noticed that the victim was a slightly built youth who bore a passing resemblance to Terry. The man handing out the beating was none other than Bart Bainbridge.

Frank put his hands to his ears as the dreaded trigger was pulled. The demonic voice urging him to 'Kill! Kill!' took charge, and an enraged Frank launched himself at the thuggish drug dealer. Blow after blow, kick after kick, landed before Bainbridge lost consciousness. Frank got on top of the thug and landed more blows before gripping him by the throat. Bainbridge would have undoubtedly met his death had it not been for the one voice that was capable of being heard and listened to over the order to 'Kill!'

It was Laura, pleading with him again and again to "Stop it! Please stop! Please stop for me!"

CHAPTER 14

Laura cradled Frank in her arms while Peter called for an ambulance. Tears ran down the tough ex-soldier's face and onto the softness of his ex-wife's blouse, as he found a moment's solace from his unforgiving world.

Laura and Peter had been visiting friends in Riverside, and the intervention had been fortuitous to put it mildly.

"An ambulance will be here in five to ten minutes," Peter said, as he motioned Laura and Frank to get into his car. After checking that Bainbridge was breathing and seemingly in no immediate danger of dying, he drove off. The youth who looked like Terry had disappeared.

The PTSD was subsiding, but Laura and Peter agreed that the best step was to take Frank back to their Richmond Road garden and give him time to deal with it, and perhaps reflect on what had occurred.

Frank had not yet heard about the egg-breaking incident, and Laura knew, and Peter insisted, that he had to be told.

However, for the moment, Frank was left to perform some deep breathing exercises before disappearing into his tent.

Peter had to pop out for a while, and Laura found herself doing some reflecting of her own.

Her first meeting with Frank at that barracks dance still resonated. She had never believed in love at first sight, and never in her wildest dreams expected to fall for someone like Frank.

Much of her childhood had been spent on the move, both in Britain and abroad, as tended to be the case with offspring of military personnel. However, as her father neared retirement, the family had a more settled existence in and around Aldershot.

By then, Laura was in her teens and by the time she was seventeen, there was a string of potential suitors. Perhaps because she wanted to avoid any more life on the move, she tended to prefer those suitors to be civilians. But there was no 'Mister Right' until the day she met Frank.

His nervous request for a dance with the then twenty two-year-old Laura was like a bolt from the blue, and she was still not sure why. He was not the tallest or best-looking man she had ever met. Nor the most erudite, for that matter. Perhaps it was a combination of piercing blue eyes and an air of vulnerability that belied a strong physique. Frank was only slightly above average height and, although pleasant-looking enough, was no matinee idol. Her parents took to him straight away, though, and it certainly helped that he could talk intelligently about military matters.

A whirlwind romance followed, with the pair meeting whenever Army commitments permitted. They soon became lovers and within a year they were husband and wife. A year after that, Terry was born.

As the wife of a soldier, she was reconciled to a life that would probably lack roots and entail long periods apart when Frank was on duty abroad. This was despite the fact that she had vowed to avoid the sort of existence her parents had experienced.

The early years were, by and large, blissful, and the couple were well able to tackle any potential test to their marriage.

It was not until Terry had approached his teens that cracks began to appear. Frank went off to fight in Iraq and, although the military engagement was brief, he was never the same again. He became distant, stayed out late almost every evening and took little interest in building on a father-son relationship that was once strong. When, some years later, Laura vainly begged Frank not to go to Afghanistan, she knew the writing was on the wall.

The once love-struck couple drifted apart, divorce followed and after meeting and eventually marrying Peter, Laura moved to a new life in Cambridge. Contact with Frank became minimal and, after she heard that Frank had left the Army because of PTSD, it became non-existent, and, for a time, Laura did not know where he was. News of Terry's death did reach Frank, however, and he was back in touch after learning of Laura's Cambridge address, which lay on file at the Aldershot Barracks.

Peter, meanwhile, had been a rock, and Laura was immeasurably relieved at the way her new husband was handling current events. Relations between Peter and Frank could have been strained and fraught. The fact that they were not could have been partly because they were both military men who basically quite liked each other.

But the way Peter was handling the difficult circumstances surrounding Frank's sudden presence in Cambridge made her increasingly aware of how Peter was always prepared to put her needs ahead of his own.

Laura readily accepted Peter's insistence that Frank must be told about the broken eggs incident. This was another example of Peter giving top priority to his wife's welfare. She decided to do this as soon as Peter returned from his brief outing, and Frank had properly cleared the latest demons in his head.

When Peter returned shortly afterwards, she told him what she planned to do, and it was not long before a more relaxed-looking Frank emerged from his tent and walked towards the house.

When Frank heard what had occurred, he was horrified and immediately offered to leave in the interests of Laura's safety. A discussion followed, and it was agreed that Frank should stay, for the time being at least, and that, between them, Peter and Frank would not allow Laura to be on her own at any time.

Laura watched with mixed emotions as the two men shook hands on the arrangement. "Let's have a cup of tea," she suggested as matter-of-factly as she could.

"Great idea!" said Frank, who then gave a start. "Oh hell! I've forgotten something! I've dropped a right royal clanger!" He told Laura and Peter about his planned visit to the John Smith Stables in Newmarket. "It completely slipped my mind! What's the matter with me?"

"I might be interested in going there myself," Laura said after a pause.

Peter suggested going over there the next day. "Why

don't you pop into town, locate Billy, tell him what's happened and then ask him to come with the three of us in my car tomorrow?" he said to Frank.

A heartfelt "Thank you" followed.

The offer that suggested Peter was an ally rather than a love rival and had been from the moment they first met was heart-warming and yet beggared belief, as far as Frank was concerned.

The search for Billy was, of course, fruitless. No one seemed to have an inkling of where he was, not even the wizened old lady with the cello.

Frank was on the point of giving up and returning to Richmond Road, when there was a tap on the shoulder and he turned to see the youth he had rescued from a beating by Bainbridge.

"Billy's got out of town," the youth said. Frank could see he was badly bruised, but at least able to move freely. "He had a ruck with Morris's right-hand man, got lucky and put him in hospital. The bloke, who I believe people call Einstein, is badly hurt and is going to be there for some time."

Before Frank could thank him properly, the youth added: "The bastard you rescued me from under the Elizabeth Way bridge is badly hurt, too. He's in hospital as well. Tommy Morris will go raving mad when he finds out!"

The John Smith Stables were accessed via a short slip road about 200 yards from Newmarket's southern outskirts. They were bounded by barbed wire fences and fronted by massive wrought iron gates. The gates, which led to a long, tree-lined lane that almost hid the main house, was manned by a security guard in a shed. The guard was tall, broad-shouldered, had a handlebar moustache and was dressed like an old-style commissionaire at a theatre or hotel. Frank got out of Peter's car and approached him. The guard's tone when he asked 'Can I help you?' was far from friendly.

"I'm looking for a stable lad called Ernie Foster, or it might be Fossey or something similar. Is he still working here?"

The guard's tone was curt and crisp. "He does, but he's not due in for another three hours."

Frank was now equally curt: "Where can I find him?"

"Try the Horse and Jockey Café. It's in the High Street, close to the Horseracing Museum," the guard said.

Without a further word, Frank returned to the car and the guard returned to his shed and picked up a telephone.

Peter agreed to drop Laura and Frank off outside the café before looking for somewhere to park, and join them in the town centre's main shopping precinct later.

The Horse and Jockey Café had a minute frontage with a grubby plate glass window. The lettering above the window was crooked and the H and Y so badly faded that they were almost invisible.

The interior consisted of a counter with a kettle, a few cakes and some cutlery and crockery on it, and a floor area with room for just two tables, some chairs and a couple of stools. The floor was covered with cheap linoleum. The stools were by a ledge that looked out onto the street.

Sitting on one of the stools was a man wearing a jockey cap, a checked shirt and jodhpurs.

"We're looking for someone called Ernie Foster, or Fossey or something like that, who works at the John Smith Stables," Frank said to the man.

The man stirred the cup of tea in front of him with a tablespoon and squinted at him suspiciously. "The name's Fosberg, Ernie Fosberg," he eventually said with a stutter. His voice was higher-pitched than Laura's. "Who's asking?"

"My name's Frank Pugsley, father of Terry Pugsley. Did my son ever work with you at the John Smith Stables?" Frank could not help observing that, although the stool Ernie Fosberg was sitting on was quite small, his feet could not touch the ground. He could only have been a jockey in days gone by, or at least an aspiring one.

"Maybe." The stable hand continued to squint.

"Let me buy you another cup of tea," Laura suggested. "How would you like another cake to go with it?"

The squint gave way to a smile and a stuttered "Thank you".

"I'm Terry's mother," Laura said, after handing over the tea and cake. "We would be really grateful if you could tell us if Terry worked with you and a bit about what he did."

"He was doing work experience," Fosberg replied, clearly embarrassed about his speech impediment. "He was a good lad. I was sorry to see him go."

"Was he popular?" Frank asked.

"Yes, everyone liked him, even the boss. If it wasn't for the drugs…"

"Go on!" urged Frank.

Ernie Fosberg suddenly looked agitated and fearful. "I've said too much already, I've got to go." He fled towards the door. The smile was long gone and he was in a state of panic.

"Who was the boss you were talking about just then?" Laura asked.

"Do you mean Dominic Hawkins, the man who owns the stables?" Frank fired the question while Ernie Fosberg was hastily exiting.

"I can't say any more."

"Is the boss Dominic Hawkins?" Frank asked again.

"I can't say any more... yes, yes, yes!"

Frank and Laura watched the red-faced stable hand half-run, half-hobble down the high street, intent only on getting away from them.

CHAPTER 15

"**Y**ou'll be lucky!" Tony Radford chuckled to himself as he watched a procession of angry campaigners calling for lower rents, march along Mill Road.

The marchers wanted more affordable homes in Cambridge and curbs on private sector landlords.

One of those landlords happened to be in a bedroom of a Victorian terraced house he had bought more than a decade ago in Mill Road and made a killing. He had spruced it up with a few licks of paint and a few improvements to the kitchen and plumbing, and found he could rent all five of its rooms for almost as much as he liked. The house was close to the corner with Ross Street, a road that once had an unenviable reputation. Radford mused over the fact that in the 1960s and early 1970s, it was said to be impossible to walk the length of Ross Street on a Saturday night without getting a black eye!

Most of the houses in the area had been built for railway workers. The area had since been 'yuppified', and Radford and others of his ilk were quids in.

The bedroom overlooking the marchers happened to be currently available, and a potential tenant, a woman in her forties who was divorced and had drink, drug and financial problems, was being given the opportunity to look at it. "There's nothing I wouldn't do for a home like this!" she had said.

Radford promised to be as accommodating as possible!

The marchers, backed by a number of politicians and trade union activists, were contending that rents in the city were becoming so high that most people could not afford them. They had congregated at Romsey Recreation Ground, and they ended up at Donkey Green, next to Parker's Piece, where there were speeches calling for more affordable council properties and help for those seeking homes in the private sector.

"Has nobody heard of payment in kind?" Radford quipped with a smirk as he unbuttoned his latest client's blouse. "There's always fun to be had if you look for it. Don't you agree?"

The woman in her forties gave him a glazed look and nodded.

"This is much more fun than getting a man with a Rottweiler to coax a late payer into coughing up!"

The rent protesters did not need a police escort, though a handful of officers were in attendance just in case. WPC Steph Shawcross was among them.

As an officer of the law, she was not allowed an opinion, of course, though she felt she had been in Cambridge for long enough to understand there was a foundation to the protest. Reports of a burgeoning economy abounded, but there were side effects.

As one of the speakers at Donkey Green said: "A lot of people in Cambridge spend a huge proportion of their earnings on rent. A third of them live in the private rented sector, and experience the highest rents outside London. Prices are going up, and ordinary people can't keep pace."

Tony Radford, meanwhile, was enjoying some of the 'fringe benefits' this particular landlord felt were his right. But he was astute enough to know that Tommy Morris was out of town, Einstein was out of action and Bob Wainwright needed to be watched. A meeting with the latter was pencilled in for later in the day, and a word of caution was to be given.

Once the demonstrators had dispersed, Steph and her patrolling colleagues headed back to the 'nick'.

Her shift for the day was nearing an end, which meant only an hour or so trying to avoid Wainwright. The inspector still wielded considerable power and made the most of his rank, though rumours about his increasingly erratic behaviour coming under scrutiny from above abounded. Steph almost preferred it when he was drunk, when it was mainly a matter of avoiding wandering hands. When he was sober, the harassment was more subtle, and was mainly by means of innuendo. Either way, his breath smelled from several feet away.

It was just a matter of time before he got a kick in the testicles!

On this occasion, Bob Wainwright was lurching along a corridor towards her.

"Hello, Steph, how about it, then?" he said as they drew nearer. His speech was more slurred than ever, his breath as foul as ever, as the inspector made a lunge and attempted to grope. "I must see a man about a dog!" he mumbled as his hands clutched nothing but air.

127

"Are you all right?" a young woman sergeant asked her, after Wainwright was gone. She was one of three people sitting in a room at the end of the corridor. "He's even more pissed than usual, it seems!"

Steph nodded: "I'm fine, though I wouldn't fancy being alone with him for any length of time."

The sergeant laughed. "I don't blame you!" The two young constables with her sat silently, and kept their counsel. Steph had chosen her words carefully. A comparative newcomer at Parkside she knew it was important to watch one's Ps and Qs. A word in the wrong place could reach the wrong ears, especially the ambitious ones.

Bob Wainwright had come to Cambridge five years ago, from the Met, where he had earned a long list of commendations. He had played a leading role in bringing several high-profile gangsters, bank robbers and drug traffickers to book, and often put himself in danger in the process. Rumour had it that some events had left Wainwright traumatised and that his transfer to Cambridge was almost akin to putting him out to pasture. None of this altered the fact that he was seen by many as a folk hero. His love of alcohol endeared him to some, and his generally wayward behaviour tended to invite the observation that he was 'only human'. Some of the rookies in the force revered him.

The young woman sergeant, whose background was in some ways similar to Steph's, was bright, attractive, always spick and span and had an air of antiseptic efficiency. She was seen as a rising star.

Well aware of Wainwright's propensities, she had a

knack of dealing with him tolerantly, tactfully and with unwavering firmness.

As Steph entered the room, she saw a diary lying open and face downwards on the floor. It bore Bob Wainwright's name. On picking it up, she glanced at a page and saw an entry that made her hair curl.

It read:

DRINKS WITH TONY, TOMMY AND DOMINIC.

The startled Steph closed the diary and put it on a desk in a corner without looking at the date of the entry, the time or venue for the meeting, or whether there was anything else on the page. She was too rattled.

"Are you OK? You look as if you've seen a ghost!" one of the young constables ventured.

"Is that Inspector Wainwright's diary you've just picked up?" the woman sergeant asked. "You don't want to be caught looking at that! It's strictly off limits! Keep well away if you know what's good for you!"

Steph could see that Wainwright was held in even more awe than she had previously thought. He was both revered and feared.

Yet she knew what she saw, and felt she would be failing in her duty if she did not speak to someone about that diary entry. Not everyone would agree, perhaps. Some might say she was meddling with something that was not her concern. But she knew she could not keep it to herself with a clear conscience. The question was: Who would willingly listen?

Frank arrived at the Leper Chapel in Newmarket Road early. He had given himself plenty of time to cycle there because he was not at all sure where it was. He was also unclear why Steph had chosen this as a rendezvous, but guessed the reason might be its remoteness.

On reaching the chapel, the oldest surviving building in Cambridge and dating from the twelfth century, he noticed a steady stream of traffic passing it on the way out of town, but no one, it seemed, actually stopping there. The railway line and a sloping downward path to a gate lay to the left of the chapel, while to the right was a paddock with three horses in it. Stone steps from the road led to a path to a door and grass to the front.

Frank had heard from Adrian and Germaine that the chapel was now home to community art, music and theatre events, including the annual re-enactment of the Stourbridge Fair. Homeless people used it to stage concerts, too.

Just now, there was no sign of life at the site at all, until an out-of-uniform Steph turned up on her bicycle.

Frank and Steph walked down the steps.

"It's an interesting spot you've chosen for us to meet," said Frank. "Are we here to say our prayers?"

"I hope not!" said Steph. "I need to talk to someone in confidence and well away from work. The Leper Chapel seems as good as any!"

"I feel flattered. Don't get me wrong. I'm not complaining, but why me and not another copper?"

She told Frank about the diary entry and the problems she was experiencing with Inspector Wainwright.

"What do you want me to do, sort the bugger out?" Frank was becoming increasingly conscious of the electricity that existed between them. "The trouble is," he added less flippantly, "that you only got a glance, you don't know the date and you can't be completely sure that Tony, Tommy and Dominic are the three people we think they are."

"I know, but it's a hell of a coincidence!" Steph sighed. "I just feel I have to do something. The real problem is that Wainwright has so much power and influence at the station, I haven't been there that long and I don't feel I can confide in anyone there."

"What about the person who's in overall charge at the nick?"

"That's Chief Constable Patterson, who's boss of the whole county, and he's hardly ever seen. The real boss at Parkside is Chief Superintendent Ellis. He's a bit remote, too, and I'm told he doesn't suffer fools gladly. He believes in doing everything by the book, but, despite his remoteness, he has a reputation for being fiercely loyal to the officers under his command."

"What, even bent ones?"

"Absolutely not! I think he would come down hard on someone who was. No one's saying Wainwright is bent, anyway, though I wouldn't be surprised if he was. It's more a matter of the way he behaves."

The pair were standing in front of a door to the chapel, which looked locked. As they walked round the side close to the paddock, Frank gently took one of Steph's hands, and Steph gave his hand a squeeze.

"I wouldn't be surprised if the super is quietly keeping tabs on things," Frank said quietly. "If he's as astute as he sounds, he will be watching Wainwright already and will jump on him if he steps out of line."

"God, I hope you're right!"

"Maybe there's a way of pushing things along a bit!"

"What do you have in mind?"

"Leave it to me, let me have a think."

Frank kissed Steph tenderly on the mouth, and Steph responded.

"What are you going to do?"

Frank ran a hand along Steph's hair and down one side of her face. "I'll think of something," he said.

Steph grabbed him by an arm after he steered her towards a spot to the side of the chapel that was surrounded by shrubs, and Frank grabbed her. Only a helicopter pilot flying low and directly above could have seen the pair lock lips and make love.

The lovemaking was the kind that began tenderly and escalated in stages to intensity and abandonment. Frank and Steph lost all sense of time, perhaps because they felt there would be no other time when they could give themselves to each other. Frank, who had yearned to be with a woman for three years, would never forget the strength of limbs that seemed intent on enwrapping him for ever and Steph's firm but womanly body. Steph half-sighed, half-screamed as she savoured the experience, at last, of being with someone other than a callow, clumsy youth.

Had it not been for the sound of someone calling to the horses in the nearby paddock, the lovemaking could have continued until infinity. Instead, Frank and Steph realised that twilight was upon them and that their idyll had to end.

A blackbird descended onto the top of the nearest shrub, looked at the couple and uttered an admonishing "Tut! Tut! Tut!"

As the couple prepared to leave, Frank looked at Steph, unsure of what best to say, before whispering: "Don't worry, everything's going to be all right!"

A tear ran down a cheek. "I hope so, darling," Steph said, half-sobbing. "I have a feeling my days in Cambridge are numbered."

CHAPTER 16

A threadbare carpet that reeked of urine and meths provided the backdrop for Tommy Morris's birth.

Lying on a settee that had seen better days was his mother, who, as always, it seemed, was stoned out of her mind. A midwife was on hand to welcome Tommy into his troubled world. But, again as always, there was no sign of the father.

Now, thirty years on, the X Factor boss, who ruled the Cambridge drugs scene with a rod of iron, was gazing from a window of a Wisbech bungalow, fascinated by the antics of a feral cat that was toying with a mouse. The bungalow belonged to his associate Tony Radford, who had handed him the keys and told him he could use it as a bolthole any time. Now was the ideal time, a time for lying low in case of a comeback over the incident when he had over-stepped himself at Tony's party.

He knew he would have to return to Cambridge soon, though. There were problems to be tackled and retribution to be administered.

The cat, which appeared to be the head of a colony that had found shelter in a ramshackle barn at the end of the back garden, was having a field day as it used a paw to knock the mouse higher and higher into the air before finally slaying and devouring it.

Tommy had not forgotten what it was like to be on the receiving end himself.

Violence had been in his veins from the word 'Go'. Even the twinkle that led to his conception was, in reality, a rape. His mother was a heroin addict, his father a latter-day Bill Sikes.

The youngest of four brothers, Tommy looked back on a life ruled by violence, abuse, heavy drinking, bullying and keeping the police and social services at bay. His mother made sure there was always food on the table and that the boys had new shoes when needed, but that was all she could manage.

The father was rarely seen. The boys were quick to learn that Friday from seven in the evening onwards was a time to lie low and stay invisible. His arrival home would be heralded by the slamming of the front door, the hurling around of whatever lay within reach, strings of expletives and a sustained beating for Mother and, quite possibly, anyone else who happened to appear on Father's radar.

When Father was not abusing Mother, he would turn his liquor-laden attention to the boys and abuse them in every way. Or he would get the boys to abuse each other.

Saturday mornings tended to be a time of relative calm, when the brothers would tiptoe downstairs and consume the cereal and fruit juice that had been left out for them the previous evening. The time Mother rose on a Saturday depended on the severity of the Friday beating.

Father would be up in time for whatever football

match was on. If he was attending an away fixture, he tended to be away himself for the rest of the weekend perhaps longer. Defeat in a home fixture was bad news for the entire household.

If Father was at home for a whole weekend, Sunday would be a day of rest or else and the rest of the family tended to disappear or, if forced to be in, move around on tiptoe while one person's much needed sleep was caught up on.

Weekdays meant school for the three other brothers, with Tommy left largely to his own devices until he reached the age of four. Mother would frequently go out in search of a 'fix' and, as soon as he could walk, Tommy would then be left locked in a room with something to eat and drink but nothing to amuse him, for anything up to five hours. Father was rarely seen, a fact that was treated as a blessing.

Unsurprisingly perhaps, school holidays were regarded by the Morris brothers as holidays for the teachers.

After reaching the age of four, Tommy was packed off to the local primary school at the earliest opportunity. By then, the two eldest brothers were at secondary school level and destined for Borstal and ten-year-old Jack was the only other brother remaining.

Jack was destined for Borstal, too. His classmates feared him, his teachers could not control him and there was talk already of sending him to an approved school.

Halfway through the year's final term, the inevitable happened. Jack, who had been running a protection racket for more than a year, was caught red-handed when the deputy head saw him administering a beating to a younger pupil who had failed to pay his 'dues'. Expulsion followed, and the teacher and many pupils sighed with relief.

As a result, Tommy was suddenly isolated and a target for bullies and cat-callers who teased him for his lisp and high-pitched voice. On his first day at school, Jack had promised to 'take him under his wing'. This had effectively meant being given lessons in how to fight dirty and not get beaten up himself as long as he helped Jack with his 'enterprise'. The help Jack required was in collecting protection money and handing out some of the beatings to late payers.

Two of the ten-year-olds regarded Jack's departure as an opportunity to exact revenge. A week later, when they felt confident that the elder brother was out of the way and under lock and key, they lay in wait after school in a lonely tree-lined lane nearby. They knew Tommy's mother rarely appeared at the school gates and that Tommy, now approaching the age of five, would be wending his way home along that lane alone.

"We're letting you off lightly because you're little," one of them said as they delivered a few slaps and gave him a black eye.

"You won't get it so easy next time, so, in future, watch it!" the other added.

On reaching home, Tommy saw Mother lying as if dead to the world on her settee, even more far gone on drugs than usual. Tommy picked up the tray carrying a slice of salami, two bread rolls and a glass of orange squash that had been left out for him and went upstairs to the bedroom, which he now had all to himself. He ate what was on offer, washed, brushed his teeth and disrobed before climbing beneath a blanket on an unmade bed and crying himself to sleep.

It was the last time Tommy ever shed a tear.

For the rest of the school term, he kept a low profile, hiding behind a shed during playtime and walking a different route to get to and from home.

The summer holidays were spent largely in isolation. Father was in prison, the two eldest brothers by then in Borstal and Jack was only allowed home for a couple of weekends. Mother made sure the boys were fed and clothed, but that was still all she could cope with. Contemporaries ostracised Tommy, sometimes at their parents' behest but more often because they were afraid of him. Much of Tommy's time was spent doing housework and going on shopping errands for Mother. The latter entailed being on the lookout for adversaries and honing his skills at stealing.

The highlights of the holiday were provided by Jack, who regaled him with tales of how he bucked the system at his approved school and was more than willing to give tips on how to fight and act tough.

During Jack's second visit, Tommy espied one of the ten-year-olds who had waylaid him on his way home during term time and told his elder brother.

"Let's follow him," Jack said.

"What are you going to do?" Tommy asked unnecessarily.

It was not long before he found out. The retribution Jack handed out, at the edge of a little used car park, led to a broken nose and jaw, the loss of six front teeth and several cracked ribs.

"This is what happens when you cross a Morris!" Jack told his victim. "Your mate will get his later! So will anyone else who gives my brother any aggro! Got it?"

By the time Tommy began his second year at school, word had got round that anyone who upset him in any way did so at their peril. The two ten-year-olds who had waylaid him the previous term had gone, and it soon became apparent that Tommy had no need to hide behind a shed or walk home in fear any more. As time went on, he became increasingly aware of the power he had over others, and by the time he was eight he was a highly dominant force.

He had become immensely strong for his age, learned about the arts of fighting and intimidation from Jack and was even feared by the ten-year-olds.

It was not long before his 'protection' business was up and running. Helping him was a new boy, whose peerless academic prowess earned him the nickname of 'Einstein'. When it came to school work, Tommy turned out to be well above average, too, and he and the boy who was to become his first lieutenant in the X Factor ran their enterprise so efficiently, ruthlessly and lucratively that none of the teachers had an inkling of what was going on.

Pupils at the secondary school where Tommy and Einstein were destined to attend had more than an inkling. Some were vengeful, but more were fearful of the Morris reputation. Father had been killed in a prison knife fight. The two elder brothers were feared inmates of another prison, while Jack ruled the roost in a Borstal the other side of the country.

One of the older boys at the school had a score to settle, though. Jack had beaten up his mate following the attack on Tommy in the tree-lined lane all those years ago. Now there was no Jack around and, reputation or no reputation, he wanted revenge. He was after Tommy's blood.

The first term was barely a week old when Einstein heard about the older boy's intentions and warned Tommy. The latter's reaction was to arm himself with a screwdriver, stolen from the woodwork room, confront his enemy in a quiet corner of a football field and stab him in the stomach and face. The older boy was rushed to hospital, where his life was saved but the use of one eye was lost.

Police enquiries into the incident met with a wall of silence. One reason was the unwritten law about not sneaking. Another was that it was made clear to pupils what would happen if the silence was broken. Some were even threatened in the presence of their parents. By then, Tommy had built up an arsenal of makeshift weapons that included nails, nail files, razor blades and safety pins. His willingness to use them was never in doubt.

Tommy Morris was still only eleven, and yet he was able to strike terror into children who were three years older. The fifteen-and sixteen-year-olds belonged to what was known as the 'upper school' and had little contact with him. When there was contact, their policy was one of circumspection.

By the time the first term was over, Tommy, Einstein and a couple of others who felt they knew which side to be on had a new 'protection' business running. As before, the teachers were kept in the dark and it was made clear what would happen if anyone dared to speak up. On one occasion, a thirteen-year-old who threatened to do so was severely beaten and hospitalised on his way home.

By the time he reached the age of thirteen himself, the power Tommy enjoyed was verging on supreme. His academic achievements continued to be above average, and his teachers predicted a bright future for him. Much of his time outside school was, in fact, spent at classes devoted to various martial arts, and he spent less time on homework than he said he did. Even the sixteen-year-olds were afraid of him. He was on the point of assuming total control.

This would have undoubtedly happened if it had not been for the death of his mother. She had been ailing for many years, she had no control over her sons, and her only solace came in the form of ever-increasing doses of heroin. In the end, her heart seemed to simply give up.

Social services were called in and Tommy was hurriedly put into care. A vacancy existed in Peterborough, which was where he was to be housed and schooled. The move made Tommy more violent and rebellious than ever, and neither the care home nor the school could control him.

Curfews and mealtimes at the former tended to be ignored altogether, with Tommy using the proceeds of thefts to eat meals out, and, as often as not, shinning up a drainpipe and climbing through his dormitory window to get in during the small hours.

Top dog in the school in Peterborough was a strapping sixteen-year-old called Oscar. A clash was inevitable and, when it happened, Oscar was left lying in a gutter half a mile from the school with his throat cut.

A spell followed at an approved school, which, again, could not contain him, and the next step was Borstal.

The hard-nosed guards and the older boys under their thumbs had heard about Tommy in advance, and accorded him the sort of welcome that was especially reserved for hard cases. The emphasis was on humiliation, with beatings, insults about his lisp and high-pitched voice, and having to do all the jobs that no one else wanted. On one occasion, a guard stood by and smirked as Tommy was subjected to a gang rape.

"It's high time you were taught a lesson," one of the guards told him on another occasion, while another gave him a shove and a kick. "You're not as tough as you thought you were, are you?"

The Borstal's top dog, Smithson watched gleefully. Once the guards had moved out of sight, Smithson sidled up to Tommy and slapped his face.

"You might think you're something at infants' school, but here you're nothing!" he snarled. "I'm top dog here and what I say goes. Got it?" Smithson delivered a second slap and repeated that Tommy Morris was nothing.

The new inmate learned his lesson quickly. He had to bide his time.

As the weeks and months went by, with Tommy keeping a low profile, the guards gradually softened their approach towards him, and even let him switch from cleaning lavatories to working in the library.

Only Smithson remained intent on humiliating him.

Tommy continued to appear cowed and subservient, knowing that his opportunity to strike back would come. The guards, who had previously watched his every move, became increasingly relaxed in their attitude towards him, allowed him more freedom of movement and instead focused on two new inmates who they felt were potentially more troublesome.

Tommy's big chance arrived when a flu epidemic struck. Half the staff fell prey to it, as did many of the boys.

One of the guards suggested the boys should be confined to their cells until staff reinforcements could be found. The deputy governor, standing in for his stricken boss, agreed and was on the point of issuing a directive to this effect when Tommy Morris struck.

Smithson decided the flu outbreak represented an opportunity for him to have an extra shower without having to seek permission first. The sight of him swaggering towards the wash house with a towel in one hand and a soap bar in the other was the last time he was seen alive.

A couple of hours later, he was found lying in a pool of blood. He had suffered multiple cuts, including several to the throat.

The atmosphere was chaotic and, although investigations were inevitable, the culprit was never found. Tommy took over as top dog and the guards were grateful that, under the new regime, chaos was kept to a minimum. Tommy's overall influence at the Borstal grew little by little, as did his muscles, until the day came for him to leave.

So it was back to Cambridge and to the next chapter in his life. The chapter began in a hostel to the north of the river. Work was hard to come by and Tommy found himself living on his wits by stealing from shops and a bit of drug dealing and mugging.

However, it was not long before his increasing

powers at the local martial arts club came to the notice of a notorious loan shark, who offered him lucrative employment. Shortly after that, he was approached by a member of the X Factor, who told him: "We're always on the lookout for fresh talent!" Such an approach was rare, and earned him instant respect among the hard men of Cambridge. The X Factor, who would not accept anyone into the fold, had access to the best drugs, and its members were guaranteed a cut of the action.

The work with the loan shark folded after a year, following a police raid that led to a long prison term for the shark.

It had been suspected, but never proved, that it was Tony Radford who had tipped the wink to the police. The shark's activities had interfered with Radford's extortionate rent-collecting activities, and Radford wanted him out of the way.

Tony Radford already owned a string of houses and flats that he let out in and around Cambridge. Some had been acquired through cheating at cards. All were at the lower end of the property market. Some of the tenants had been victims of his own loan-sharking. Some were drug addicts in need of loans to finance their habit, and, in one way or other, Radford seemed to have power over all of them.

A few of the tenants were becoming rebellious, though, and it became apparent that some extra 'enforcement muscle' was needed. Tommy Morris fitted the bill perfectly.

By the time Tony Radford approached him, Tommy had taken over as head of the X Factor. The previous leader, then forty, had died suddenly of a heart attack, and his second in command found he was wrong in assuming he could automatically take over the reins. Tommy, who had re-established contact with Einstein and quietly built up a following of his own, ended up on top in a ferocious battle that ended with his rival suffering near-fatal injuries and being totally broken.

The unwritten, unofficial partnership between Tony Radford and Tommy Morris was of immense mutual benefit. For the former, there was formidable muscle on hand whenever needed. For the latter, the need to live in a hostel was very much a thing of the past.

As Tommy looked out onto the Wisbech garden, he reflected on the fact that, until recently, he could feel he had it all sewn up.

He had probably got away with what he did at Tony's party, though the presence of a policeman, even a 'tame' one, caused him unease. He had decided to get away for a while until any possible hubbub had died down.

But there were other worries. Einstein, his first lieutenant, had been badly hurt and would be out of action for some time. The same had happened to Bart Bainbridge, his newest recruit. To make matters worse, two other X Factor members had gone. One had been jailed after a fracas at a football match. The other had simply dropped out.

To add to Tommy's worries, there had been reports of a gang of Albanian sex slave traffickers moving to Cambridge and potentially taking an interest in the drugs trade.

So there were X Factor replacements to be sought and investigations into the Albanian rumour to be carried out.

Much of the trouble had, of course, been caused by Terry Pugsley's father. He had to be dealt with, too.

CHAPTER 17

Christ's pieces may not be everyone's first choice as a place to sit and reflect, but that's where Frank found himself just after the crack of dawn.

Confused, unable to sleep and yet strangely serene, the only certainty in his mind was that he was right to have come to Cambridge. Since his arrival, though, he had found himself confronted with more questions than answers. He remained convinced that there was more about the death of his son, Terry, than met the eye, but unsure what to do next. He felt the need to reflect on his unplanned tryst with Steph, as well.

Frank gazed across the area of parkland that separated the city centre with all its colleges from the more humdrum Grafton Centre. On one side of the 'Piece' was King Street, on the other a bustling but somewhat chaotic bus station. Tennis courts and bowling greens were among the attractions.

The bench he was sitting on was still damp with dew. The park's feathered inhabitants were well into their dawn chorus, and half a dozen or so dogs could be seen gambolling on the grass while their rough-sleeping owners remained largely inert. The dogs sported glossy coats, exuded wellbeing and looked far better cared for than their owners. Shop workers, mainly in ones and twos, traversed the path that connected the two distinctly different parts of Cambridge to get to their jobs.

What really happened to Terry? Frank asked himself for the umpteenth time.

Why was it that everyone seemed afraid to talk about Terry's death? Why was it that, when he appeared to be on the verge of obtaining information, the trail went cold? At the very least, he wanted to nail the dealer who was responsible for Terry taking that fatal overdose.

Frank reflected on the sudden death of the drug dealer Toby, the hasty departure of Billy and the way the stable hand Ernie had fled from that Newmarket café in fright. Laura and Peter had commented on this, too. What was the part, assuming he had one, that Tony Radford had in all this? And why did Ernie say Dominic Hawkins knew Terry when the respected auctioneer said he did not? Hawkins had a lot of people in his employ, of course, and it could be that he did not know every work experience employee who passed through his hands by name. But this still needed to be looked into.

On top of all this, there was ambivalence in his feelings for Steph. Laura had been, and still was, the love of his life, and, given the chance, he would have had her back at the drop of a hat. But, as things stood, there appeared to be no chance at all. The electricity between the forty-year-old ex-soldier and the much younger WPC had been instant. But did that justify what had happened at the Leper Chapel? Yet another matter to be resolved was his pledge to help her deal with the odious Inspector Wainwright. The promise had been made in the heat of the moment, but, in reality, he had no idea what to do at all.

Perhaps a workout will shake up those brain cells! Having come to that conclusion, Frank picked up his kit bag, mounted his bike and headed towards the sports centre.

As he reached the roadside, he saw a Porsche draw up and a young man with a straggly beard emerge and head for the area he had just left. He was wearing Army surplus clothes and a cloth cap and was carrying a placard with words that included 'PLEASE HELP' on it. The woman at the wheel drove off.

"I wonder if he's one of those bogus beggars that the newspapers keep talking about?" Frank wondered.

As he reached the sports centre a quarter of an hour before it was due to open, he opted for an outdoor warm-up consisting of a run to the Mill Road bridge and back, twenty star jumps and a dozen press-ups.

The weight training room was a hive of activity from the word go. Two young women busied themselves on trampolines and talked about their office's impending fun run. Two young men were flexing their biceps in front of mirrors, a pensioner was gingerly doing a set of curls, and the various weight machines were being taken up minute by minute.

In one corner were two man mountains, one aged about twenty, the other thirty or so. Both were clad in sleeveless tops that revealed massive upper arms and garish tattoos, and they both looked vicious. Frank could sense that they were looking at him, and his skin crawled.

148

The tattooed men spoke in hushed tones, but Frank had an acute sense of hearing and was also adept at lip-reading.

"Best we leave him be 'til we get the word," the older of the two could be heard to say.

The younger one nodded. "What's the latest on Einstein?" he asked.

"In a bad way. He'll be out of action for a long time."

"What about the guv'nor? Haven't seen him lately."

The older man put a finger to his lips. The conversion ceased to be audible, and within minutes the pair were gone.

The older of the two man mountains got into a car that had been parked beneath the hall and drove off.

The younger one crossed Mill Road and began to saunter across a grassy area that accessed East Road.

"I want words with you!" a voice could be heard from behind. The muscle man turned to see he had been followed by Frank Pugsley.

"You belong to Tommy Morris's gang, don't you?" Frank said.

The younger man, who towered over Frank, snarled, "What if I do?"

"I have some questions to ask you."

"You're quite right, I am in Tommy's gang. I'm a member of the X Factor, and that means you need to be careful!"

"Or what?"

"You're really asking for it, aren't you?"

Frank responded by slapping the young man's face.

The latter aimed a kick at Frank's left kneecap, and,

had it not been for Frank's lightning reflexes, the kick would have landed and disabled him. A succession of kicks, punches, thumb thrusts and parries by both men followed until, finally, Frank brought the young man to his knees with a blow to the solar plexus.

"You know who I am, don't you?" Frank said as he stood over the man he had felled. "Don't you!" he repeated while delivering a finger jab to the neck that made his adversary yelp.

The muscular young man nodded.

"I want to know how my son died. Did you have anything to do with it?" The young man was made to yelp again for failing to answer. "Tell me, or I will kill you!"

"No, it was nothing to do with me."

"Was Tony Radford involved?"

"No, at least I don't think so."

"What about Tommy Morris?"

"If I say anything against Tommy, he will kill me!"

Frank made him yelp again. "If you don't tell me what I want to know, I will kill you! Do Morris and Radford work together?"

"Yes, they sort of help each other out."

"Did Radford have anything to do with the death of my son?"

"No, not as far as I know. I don't know anything about this."

"What about Morris? Answer me, or I'll take you apart!"

"All right, yes yes yes! I don't know any details, though. And if Morris finds out I've been talking to you, he'll kill me!"

"Did you know about my son working at the John Smith Stables in Newmarket?"

Frank was all set to deliver another finger jab for failure to answer a question, when he heard an "Oi!" from an upstairs window of a nearby house. A young couple then came into view and began to cross the grass.

The vanquished young thug struggled to his feet and half-sauntered, half-staggered towards East Road, while Frank sat on a bench and pondered. He could not believe how composed he felt, with his head filled with rational thought and not a hint of that dreaded voice!

After some deliberation, he decided to head back to Christ's Pieces. As he went to collect his bike, he espied a small stall that had just been put up outside the sports centre entrance. He saw that 'instamatic' cameras were for sale and felt it would be amusing to buy one. A picture or two of the homeless men and women with their handsome dogs might lighten the day.

Some of the dogs were still frolicking on his return. Some were sitting serenely with their masters and mistresses, who had now formed a group in one corner. French, German, Hispanic, Eastern European and oriental tongues could be heard from language students, who were sitting in clusters on the lush green grass. The diagonal path that ran from one corner of Christ's Pieces to another saw pedestrians and cyclists move to and from the city centre.

One of the few people to be sitting alone was the young man with the straggly beard, who was occupying a bench and displaying his placard. Frank could now read all the words:

PLEASE HELP. I HAVE NO HOME AND HAVE NOT
EATEN FOR TWO DAYS.

The cloth cap, held to the ground by a few pieces of silver and copper, lay at his feet.

Frank made his way towards the group with their dogs. He knew some of the faces, and was greeted warmly. The members of the group all knew him or at least knew of him.

"Hi there!" one of the men said. "How are you doing?"

"You're Frank Pugsley, aren't you?" a skinny, middle-aged woman with a sallow complexion asked. "I've heard about you."

"Not all bad, I hope!" Frank quipped.

"No, it's been all good," another man said.

"Thank you. It's good to see you, too," Frank replied, who, consumed with curiosity, then turned towards the man with the straggly beard. "Have you any idea who that geezer is?"

"We don't know who he is, but we have a fair idea of what he's up to," the first man, a young Geordie with rosy cheeks and a beer paunch, said. "We reckon he's a phoney."

"He's been sniffing around for the last two or three days, and we reckon he's after easy pickings in Cambridge," a lanky young Irishman volunteered.

"I've a good mind to go over there and kick his teeth in!" a diminutive Brummie, who moved with a limp and was almost certainly nudging fifty, added.

The conversation continued in the same vein for several minutes and would have lasted longer had it not been for the arrival at Christ's Pieces of a familiar figure.

All eyes were focused on the bulky form of inspector Bob Wainwright, who was clad in a crumpled blue suit and was tottering along the path towards the Grafton Centre. He was lurching from left to right and back again, causing alarm to others who happened to be in his path.

Without warning, he unzipped his trousers and urinated on the path directly in front of a group of young Swiss girls and shouted a string of French expletives.

By then, Frank's camera was working overtime.

A moment later, the inebriated Inspector saw the young man with the straggly beard, lurched over to him and tossed a £20 note into the gaping cloth cap. He then staggered in the general direction of Parkside, leaned over a hedge and vomited into someone's garden.

Meanwhile, the man with the straggly beard could not believe his luck. Almost immediately after he had pocketed the £20 note, a group of well-heeled language students approached him, dipped into their purses and pockets and plied him with monetary notes. One of the notes was worth £50, not the £5 that the student thought.

Once the group had gone, the bearded man reached for his mobile phone and spoke into it gleefully. He walked triumphantly towards the nearest road, and the Porsche that had ferried him to Christ's Pieces earlier on reappeared. A young woman in a designer dress and coiffured hair got out of the car, embraced the young man and offered her congratulations.

As she did so, the redoubtable Inspector Wainwright collided with the couple, burped loudly and continued his wayward walk to wherever he thought he was going.

That must be the star turn to end all star turns! Frank

thought as he put his camera away. *Our policeman friend has done enough to earn himself an Oscar, though the bogus beggar can't be far behind!*

Perhaps the new chief of police should be the one to judge

CHAPTER 18

"WHAT CAN I DO for you as if I didn't know?" the station sergeant asked with the most knowing of looks. It was the same avuncular sergeant who had greeted him on his first visit, after he had helped apprehend the notorious Rick O'Reilly.

Frank managed to smile. "Does that mean I'm going to have to make a run for it?" he quipped.

"Not at all, sir," the chuckling sergeant behind the counter said. "We were worried about you before, and it's good to see you're all right."

"I'm fine, thanks. Is it possible to speak to Steph, or perhaps I should say WPC Shawcross?"

The sergeant made some enquiries and told Frank that she was out on a job, but he promised to let her know he had called round.

"She's a bright girl, isn't she?" said Frank.

"Yes, she's a bright girl with a bright future," the sergeant agreed. "We'll be sorry to lose her."

Frank gave a start. "I didn't know she was leaving."

The sergeant faltered for a moment before replying: "I didn't mean she was going right now, but a young officer with a good academic record, especially a degree, tends to get moved around a lot to gain experience and quite possibly be fast-tracked to promotion."

Frank decided it would be prudent to change the subject, and referred to the recently reported change of command in the county's police force. "I hear you're about to get a new chief."

"That's right," the sergeant said. "Patterson has retired as Chief Constable for Cambridgeshire, and Mackenzie is due to start here tomorrow."

"Will the change at the top mean changes at the nick?"

"Now you're asking!" The sergeant rubbed his chin and looked at Frank speculatively. "Let me say this: The new man, Crawford Mackenzie, demands that everything is done by the book. He's a stickler for rules and he's as straight as a die. The same goes for Chief Superintendent Ellis."

"So anyone who bends the rules will be in trouble?"

"You said that, not me!" The smile had gone and the reply was curt, bordering on defensive. "You will have to excuse me, there's something I must attend to," he added, before disappearing through a door at the side.

Frank had considered handing to the sergeant the parcel he had brought along for Steph and asking him to hand it over when he saw her. Now he decided to take it to the Post Office and send it to the Chief Constable personally by Special Delivery.

Next on Frank's agenda were visits to Radford and Hawkins, two men who belonged to opposite ends of the property spectrum. One had a reputation for sleazy dealings, the other for being a pillar of respectability. He had questions for both of them, even though they were poles apart. There were questions, too, for the formidable Morris, who was nowhere to be seen just now. However, Frank was well aware that they were destined to meet again and that a violent confrontation was inevitable.

He was out of luck. The calls on the two Cambridge offices led to two virtually identical responses: "I'm afraid he's out and he's unlikely to be back for some time."

He knew that Laura and Peter were keen to have answers, too, and was on the point of leaving the centrally located Regent Street and heading back to Richmond Road to discuss with them what to do next, when he saw a familiar bulky form a hundred or so yards away disappear down a side street near the imposing Roman Catholic church.

Bob Wainwright's head was beginning to clear. He was beginning to realise he had put his size twelve in it in a big way, and was clinging to the hope that his actions on Christ's Pieces did not come to the notice of colleagues. He gazed towards the church entrance and then upwards at the roof, as if to seek a spiritual explanation for his crass behaviour.

He did not find one and, in truth, did not really want one. He was heading for the nearest hostelry to meet Tony Radford and seek liquid salvation.

The once high-flying police inspector was, even in his worst moments, conscious of how he had plummeted to the depths, though. His life was on the verge of spiralling out of control, and there seemed to be nothing he could do about it. The once youthful Inspector Bob Wainwright, fabled crime-busting hero of the Met, had been the subject of speculation that a glittering future lay ahead of him, with promotion to the rank of chief constable somewhere at the very least.

Some of his exploits had got into the press, and he was arguably the only policeman in the land who could be hailed as a folk hero.

One of his most fabled heroic deeds was to infiltrate a feared East London gang of protection racketeers, drug dealers and sex-traffickers. To gain the leader's trust, he had to witness and even take part in violent beatings to people who had incurred his displeasure, or take part in illegal transactions. Eventually, and at great risk to himself, he was able to lure the gang into a dockland meeting involving handing over money for drugs from Colombian dealers, while police were lying in wait. As a result of the trap and evidence Bob Wainwright had garnered about other crimes, the ringleaders and most of the other gang members were jailed for a long time.

Another exploit involved the break-up of a vice ring. The young policeman was undercover again, but on this occasion one of the pimps became suspicious and attacked him with a knife and a fight to the death ensued.

In another, he disarmed and apprehended two bank robbers wielding revolvers and crowbars.

Yet another commendation was conferred on Inspector Wainwright, whose courage, skills of detection and ability to react quickly in any situation were becoming increasingly noticed by the police force's top brass.

What was not noticed, for some time at any rate, was the rising star's reliance on alcohol. Initially, the ability to hold liquor was often part and parcel of gaining respect and confidence among some of the gangland figures. Later on, a stiff drink was the way to water down the effects of what he had had to see and do.

And then, inevitably perhaps, the drink took over and he had to rely on it, no matter what. His behaviour became increasingly irrational, his marriage disintegrated and he began to be regarded as a loose cannon. The powers that be eventually recognised the severity of the problem and sent him to a 'drying-out centre'.

After three months at the centre and another couple of weeks' leave, he was offered a post in Cambridge – a 'backwater' best known for its halls of learning and allegedly free of heavy-duty violence.

The head of the county force, Patrick Patterson had done his best to be accommodating, and the inspector had enjoyed being looked up to by so many of the younger officers.

Unfortunately, however, Mackenzie was on his way now and he knew what to expect.

Among those who knew of Bob Wainwright's reputation was Tony Radford, who had initially been consumed with feelings, in equal measure, of awe and envy. Before long, these feelings had given way to pride at having a man of Wainwright's calibre as an ally. And, a little after that, it dawned on him that Wainwright was not the man he once was and that he could even exert a degree of power over the policeman.

But now Tony Radford was worried. Bob Wainwright seemed to be permanently inebriated, and his behaviour was becoming increasingly outlandish. A 'tame' policeman in a tight ship could be a major asset. But a loose cannon, which he was fast becoming, was a liability.

To make matters worse, Tommy Morris had temporarily disappeared and the X Factor had been losing members. With advancing age, Radford was becoming increasingly reliant on the X Factor for 'enforcement duties.'

He had just struck a new deal with Lee Bains that had again entailed buying up a parcel of land with several properties on it that were to be demolished and replaced by a block of new flats. The problem was that two houses were occupied and the tenants living in them had to be persuaded to leave. There had been a time when Radford had no qualms about going round on his own with a Rottweiler and scaring the tenants away.

What he wanted now was a bit of help with the 'leaning on' process, but, in the absence of Morris and his first lieutenant Einstein, he did not know where to find it.

What he did not know yet was that Bob Wainwright, who had been reliably and discreetly turning a blind eye on some of his dealings for 'a consideration', was about to demand further recompense for his discretion.

Tony Radford's feelings for the inspector, his drinking buddy, with the heroic track record, had become laced with contempt.

There were no epic exploits in the past he could point to, only sleaze. His parents, now dead, had resided on a council estate and largely lived off the state. What little income they had was augmented from time to time with the proceeds of petty thefts and various dodgy deals some leading to terms in prison. Tony Radford Sr had died of cirrhosis of the liver at the age of fifty, while mother Margaret met her death a few years later in a traffic accident.

Meanwhile, Tony's only sibling, Kirsty, eight years his senior, was languishing in Holloway Prison. A former escort girl who fleeced clients at every opportunity, she had been jailed for stabbing and killing a man who had caught her rifling through his belongings while she thought he was asleep.

Yet, despite all these disadvantages in life, Tony was doing all right. He owned a string of properties in and around Cambridge, drove around in a Porsche or an MG, depending on his mood, and ran the second biggest estate agency in town.

One of the two main reasons why the younger Tony prospered while other family members failed was, quite simply, his ability to steal and arrange dodgy deals without getting caught. The other was sheer luck.

At the age of twenty, he bet £20 on a rank outsider in a high-profile horse race at Aintree and won £600 when the two joint favourites fell and the outsider romped home. A few days later, his ability to cheat at poker netted him winnings worth £2,000. His unsuspecting victim, an eighteen-year-old who had just left the Perse School, could only come up with half of this, and, fearful of incurring the wrath of his father if found to have been gambling, agreed to transfer ownership of a flat he had just inherited to Tony as long as he could continue to use one of the rooms.

The flat was worth considerably more than the total gambling debt, of course, and Tony, with the aid of the

£600 win and the proceeds of various thefts and scams was able to form the basis of his property empire.

The flat contained three bedrooms and, with the ex-Perse boy at university in Plymouth, Tony made sure all three rooms were constantly let at the highest rent he could get away with. The ex-Perse boy's father died and his mother's failing health rendered her unwilling or unable to question what had been going on.

A couple of years later, an uncle whom Tony Radford hardly knew but who had no other relatives, bequeathed his estate in two equal portions to Tony and his sister. The main part of the estate consisted of two terraced houses in Chesterton Fen and, with his sister in jail, Tony wasted no time in making them further sources of rental income.

Places to rent in Cambridge were in desperately short supply and the properties were all constantly packed with people prepared to accept virtually any terms as long as they had somewhere to live.

It was not long before another house-buying opportunity arose, when a couple found themselves unable to continue with their mortgage repayments, the mortgage lender took over the property and put it back on the market. It turned out to be a 'snip' for Radford, who bought it at an auction, refurbished it a little and sold it on for a handsome profit... which was used to buy two more flats.

Further opportunities of that nature arose from time to time and, within ten years, the Radford property portfolio consisted of twenty houses and flats, most of them in Cambridge and all in East Anglia. Establishing an estate agency business, which was to include house sales as well later, looked like a logical extension, and this separate business burgeoned rapidly.

As a young man, Tony Radford cut an intimidating figure, and the fear factor was adeptly used to augment his entrepreneurial skills.

As he grew older and less able to execute threats personally, he increasingly appreciated the liaison he had managed to establish with Morris.

And then, two years ago, there was his chance meeting with Bob Wainwright, which was to be the icing on the cake. The pair happened to be propping up the same bar in a pub near the police station and they hit it off immediately, though all they had in common was being burly and physically past their best.

The astute Tony Radford, impressed with the tales he had heard about Bob Wainwright's past, instinctively knew, after a while, that he could manipulate the policeman. By plying him with whisky and vodka, he inveigled Wainwright into giving a detailed description of his life story and, in particular, how he became dependent on alcohol.

The pair agreed to meet up again and, little by little, Radford was able to get Wainwright to turn a blind eye to his activities and, later, to those of Tommy Morris.

Tony Radford seemed to have it all sewn up. With the backing of Morris's muscle and a 'tame copper', he felt he could do more or less exactly what he liked. Until now...

Apart from Morris going missing and Wainwright's reliability becoming increasingly questionable, a clampdown on exorbitant letting fees charged to tenants was being planned by Chancellor Philip Hammond. This was something that could seriously impinge on a lucrative part of his business empire.

All these thoughts were racing through his mind as he bestrode a bar stool and waited. What was he going to say? Was a beautiful friendship about to end?

The imminence of an answer was heralded by the sound of a door flying open, and a half-stumbling Bob Wainwright waved a hand and lurched towards the stool. "Hiya, Tony! I hope you haven't drunk the place dry! I have a thirst!" he roared.

Tony bought a couple of whiskies and pointed towards a corner. "Let's go over there. We can get stoned discreetly there!" he said with a wry smile.

As they moved towards the corner, a new arrival approached the bar unnoticed and bought a half of bitter.

"How are things?" Tony asked his companion.

"I'm worried."

"Why's that?"

Bob Wainwright described the change that was taking place at the top in the county's police force.

The property baron paused and scratched his tummy. "I think we're going to have to knock things off for a bit," he said gravely "…at least until things have settled down a bit and we've had a chance to see the lie of the land."

"Does that mean we have to stay sober, too?"

The two men both sensed that a degree of friction was afoot.

"Perhaps we should not be seen together for a while," Tony Radford suggested.

"Hmff!" Bob Wainwright looked mortified, but

reluctantly saw the logic. "OK, if you say so but how about a bit of the readies, in the meantime?"

The flashpoint had arrived.

"What for?"

"What do you mean 'What for?'. For services rendered, of course!"

After a sharp intake of breath, the Radford response was: "You got a tidy sum off me the last time. What have you done to make me add to it since then?"

Bob Wainwright went purple. "Why, you…!"

Radford rose to his feet, told the errant policeman to calm down and left hurriedly.

"All right, be like that!" Wainwright bellowed before he could reach the door. "I'll be having words with your toffee-nosed friend about this, and we'll see what he has to say!"

As Tony Radford headed back towards Hills Road and the church, he heard footsteps behind him and felt a tap on the shoulder. He turned to see a man who was smaller but looked stronger than he was.

"You're Tony Radford, aren't you?" Frank asked him.

"Who wants to know?"

"The name's Pugsley. Does that ring any bells?"

"Why should it?"

"I'm the father of Terry Pugsley, who died recently of a massive drugs overdose. Perhaps you remember now. What have you got to say about that?"

"What's that got to do with me?"

Frank felt the anger welling up in him. He did not know the extent of Radford's involvement, but he knew he was in the mix somewhere.

"You will be telling me next you have never heard of Tommy Morris!"

"I have no idea what you're talking about. Go to hell!"

Unable to contain his anger any longer, Frank felled Radford with a right-hander to the jaw. "Tell me what I want to know or I'll do you!" he screamed.

The man on the ground went puce. "I don't know anything. I can't help you!" he wailed.

Frank, who had enjoyed a period of comparative serenity of late, was about to deliver a slap when the dreaded trigger went off and the demonic voice took over. "Kill, kill!" it demanded.

Tony Radford, sensing that something was making his tormentor back off, struggled to his feet and fled as fast as his flabby frame would permit.

CHAPTER 19

Tranquility was the attraction of Laura and Peter's back garden later that day. Frank felt the need to reflect and fill his mind with all that was beautiful, cerebral and free of conflict. His cycle ride up Castle Hill and Huntingdon Road and along the leafy-lined Richmond Road had done much to help the calming process already. On reaching the house, he knocked on the front door once, went round the side and, on seeing Laura from the corner of an eye, offered a perfunctory wave.

Now he was sitting outside his tent, savouring the setting he was in. A small pond, from which frogs would intermittently emerge and then submerge themselves again, held his gaze until he saw a hedgehog scuttle from one fence to another and disappear under a bush. A blackbird was splashing about in a raised stone bath. Two chaffinches were pecking at the grain that had been left in a small hanging basket. A robin was sitting on a fence post, sending out the strident message that this was his territory and his alone. Bees were busying themselves around buds, and a red admiral butterfly was proudly displaying its magnificent colouring.

Laura was watching from the kitchen window. If there was anyone who knew what was going through Frank's mind at any time it was Laura. One thing she knew for sure was that at this particular moment, he needed space. She was as aware as anyone could be that Frank would come out of his private world and return to the world inhabited by others in his own good time.

She was able to reflect, however, that there had been good times aplenty when she and Frank were together.

There was the day when it had been arranged she would meet Frank at Harwich for a short outing and, to her amazement, found they had been booked on a voyage to Norway and a tour of the fjords. The moment when, with smiling eyes, Frank handed over her passport, which he had somehow managed to get hold of unseen, was as vivid as ever.

Equally memorable was their time in the Lake District, when Frank erected a tent beside Red Tarn and, after a night of sheer bliss under canvas, took her to the top of Helvellyn via Striding Edge.

A trip on a Venetian gondola, a train ride through the Canadian Rockies and swims from various sun-kissed beaches in Britain and abroad were among the other magical moments.

The most abiding memory of all, though, was the birth of Terry in a Bristol hospital, his early upbringing and all the signs of a father-son bonding that could not be surpassed.

It was not until Terry approached his teens that things started to go wrong. Laura's parents died within a year of each other, Frank seemed to be more and more married to the Army rather than to her, and then Terry started to go off the rails. She began to appreciate that there could be truth in the saying that misfortunes had a way of arriving in threes, though, in her case, it was in fours.

She shuddered to think what might have transpired if, within a year of her splitting up with Frank, she had not met Peter. Here was a man who, without doubt, became Peter the rock!

The strident sound of the front doorbell brought Laura back to the present. Standing outside was an athletic-looking young woman with fair hair. "I understand Frank Pugsley lives here," she said. "Would it be possible to have a word with him?"

"Yes, I'm sure you can. Can I ask who I am speaking to?"

"My name's Stephanie Shawcross. I'm the policewoman who Mr Pugsley helped to arrest a troublemaker in the city centre. I am very grateful to him, and I now have something to tell him."

Laura's first instinct was to say Frank was busy. But she decided this would be churlish and she took the new arrival round the side.

"There's a visitor for you," she called out on reaching the garden. "A Miss Shawcross."

Frank rose to his feet.

"I'll leave you to it," Laura said, before going inside.

Frank and Steph stared at each other, transfixed for a few seconds, before Frank broke the silence. "Did you get the message that I'd called round the nick?"

"Yes, sure. I would have got back to you earlier, but there's been a lot of stuff going on."

"What do you mean? Are you still having trouble with slime ball Wainwright?"

Steph faltered for a second. "No, at least not any more by the looks of it."

"That sounds good. What's happened?"

"I'm not sure what's happened, to be honest, but something's been going on and I've heard a whisper that the slime ball has been suspended."

Frank tried to look surprised. "How come?"

Steph stroked her hair and rubbed her nose. "This is the tricky bit. I don't really know, and can only go on hearsay..."

"Come on, put me out of my misery!" Frank's tone was verging on impatience. "You're being very mysterious!"

"OK, it's something like this. A new chief constable by the name of Mackenzie has just arrived and, almost as soon as he set foot in the station at Parkside, he was involved in lots of hushed conversations..."

"Go on."

"Well, it seems as if someone's tipped him the wink about some of the things Wainwright's been up to. The last time I saw the slime ball was yesterday, when, as soon as he arrived, he was summoned to see the new boss."

"Was he now! And what happened then?"

"I'm not sure. Someone saw him skulking out of the back of the building, and no one has seen him since."

"That's interesting, but what makes you think he's suspended?"

Steph rubbed her nose again. "Only what I've heard. An inspector and a sergeant were talking in hushed tones in a corner, and I'm almost certain I heard the words

'Wainwright's in for the high jump!' mentioned in the same sentence. Apart from that, there is a strong feeling among colleagues generally that this is what has happened. So it looks as if you won't have to do anything to sort him out!"

Frank was unable to suppress a smile. "It certainly sounds like it and, let's face it, that's great news! You must be feeling relieved, to say the least."

The smile was not returned, however, and it suddenly dawned on Frank that the news about Wainwright was by no means the main purpose of her visit.

"I'm relieved to a point," Steph said at length, "though what has happened does not really affect me."

Frank's mind went back to what she had said during their tryst at the Leper Chapel, and he knew what was coming next. "So you're on the move, then?"

Steph looked at the ground and sighed. "Yes, I'm about to be stationed at Billericay. I'm not sure, but I think Wainwright had something to do with this. I had once heard him saying on the phone to someone that I did not really fit in at Parkside… no prizes for guessing why he said that… and the old chief, Patterson, rubber-stamped the move."

"Why would the slime ball do that?" Was he really that vindictive?"

"It looks that way, a case of dented pride I guess! When Wainwright realised that I did not welcome his attentions, he took offence, said things behind my back and put it about that my future with the police ought to be elsewhere. As it happens, the Billericay job is mainly about community policing, which is something that appeals to me."

"Good grief! When do you start?"

"I'll be gone in a couple of days."

Neither Frank nor Steph were sure what to say next.

"It sounds as if you've fallen on your feet," Frank eventually said. "I hope we can stay in touch."

Steph went red, and she gazed at the ground. Then she looked up and directly into Frank's eyes. "I don't think so," she replied haltingly. "There's no future for you and I, is there? Let's be honest. You're still in love with your ex-wife, aren't you?"

Frank watched as the young WPC turned without waiting for an answer and headed hurriedly towards the street.

"She's just twenty-two and has a far older head than I have!" he murmured to himself.

Laura was watching, too, as well as wondering. There was plenty she wanted to talk about already, with points to be put and questions asked. Peter, who was out at the time, was increasingly wanting to become involved in what was going on, and a 'summit' at the Andrews' household had become a must.

As Steph cycled homewards, and seemingly out of Frank's life for ever, Bob Wainwright brought a halt to his latest binge, returned to his flat and began to consider what life would be like outside the force. He was beginning to appreciate the enormity of his situation, and that the writing was almost certainly on the wall.

The beleaguered police inspector reached for his telephone and asked to speak to the one person he thought might be able to get him out of the mire.

"Mr Hawkins can see you in his office at seven-thirty this evening," a woman with clipped tones told him after a seemingly endless pause.

Dominic Hawkins, slim and elegant as ever, was standing just inside the front door when Bob Wainwright arrived. He led him into and through a darkened building to the palatial room that served as his base. After motioning his guest towards a chair close to his monolith of a desk, the up-market estate agent and auctioneer who appeared to have everything picked up a handsome wooden box containing Havana cigars and offered one to his guest. The offer was accepted readily.

He then picked up the gavel that doubled up as a lighter and provided the necessary flame. Bob Wainwright's look of surprise was no surprise to him.

"You've already seen my collection of gavels, haven't you," Hawkins said. "The collection is my pride and joy, and I value it even more than I do my racehorses."

"They must be gold-plated!" Wainwright exclaimed.

"Not all of them!" chuckled Hawkins. "No, the reason I value them is that every gavel in my collection has a dual purpose. They're not just used to herald the close of sales at auctions."

Wainwright stared in amazement.

"As you know, one of them doubles up as a lighter. Let me show you what another one can do."

Dominic Hawkins ran a hand along the line of implements that stood in an orderly line on his desk and picked up one with an ivory handle. He pointed one end towards a cork mat used for pictures on a wall, pressed a button and an open-mouthed Wainwright saw a knife fly through the air and pierce the mat.

Wainwright was at a loss for words.

Hawkins laughed loudly. "Anyway, I'm sure you haven't come here to admire my eccentric collecting habits. What can I do for you?"

Wainwright faltered, before mumbling that he was "in a spot of bother and could do with some readies".

Hawkins removed the knife from the mat, put it back inside the gavel and laid down the latter precisely where it was before.

"You certainly have your uses, don't you?" he said, his smile now gone.

"I like to think so."

"What you are particularly good at is turning a blind eye to things. Isn't that so?"

Wainwright nodded.

"The ability to turn a blind eye is definitely something to be valued… as long as there is one person around who keeps his eyes open; it wouldn't do if we were all blind." Hawkins paused, rose from his chair and went to the drinks cabinet. "I must apologise. Please have a whisky. I meant to offer you one before, but became so absorbed with my gavels that I completely forgot. I must appear very rude."

Hawkins poured some whisky into a large glass and handed the drink to his visitor. "There you go, drink up!"

Wainwright took a hesitant sip and then, knowing what was expected of him, gulped down the rest of the drink with gusto.

"My goodness, you made short work of that! Have another!" Hawkins re-filled the glass and asked: "Is it cash you need?"

Wainwright nodded. "I just need something to tide me over for a while."

"No problem!" Hawkins assured him. "All I need to be sure of is that you know how to be discreet. As I have already said, I put great value on the ability to turn a blind eye."

"I really appreciate what you're doing," Wainwright mumbled before emptying the contents of the whisky glass again.

"That's excellent! I'm a man who really appreciates appreciation!"

Wainwright began to laugh. Then suddenly, he put his hands to his head and announced that he felt sick.

"My dear fellow!" Hawkins exclaimed. "Are you all right? You've gone green!"

"I feel funny!" said Wainwright.

"I'm so sorry! The whisky must have a bigger kick to it than I thought! You should probably go home and lie down, though you're clearly in no fit state to drive."

Wainwright somehow managed to get to his feet.

"Don't worry, old boy, I'll drive you home," said Hawkins. "It's the least I can do."

CHAPTER 20

"Einstein's on his way out!"

"What do you mean 'On his way out?' Is 'e dying or somefink?"

"Nope. I mean e's leaving Cambridge. So's Bainbridge."

"How come?"

"They've 'ad enough. It looks like they've been finding fings too 'ot for 'em since Frank Pugsley turned up."

"They're not the only ones. Another one's fled with cold feet and another's getting married and ain't interested any more."

"It looks like Tommy Morris could be losing his powers."

It was first thing Saturday morning and a group of around half a dozen homeless men were sitting in a huddle in a remote part of the Lion Yard's multi-storey car park. As always, they had expressed relief at having survived another dreaded Friday night, a time when many of those with homes to go to knew that the city centre was not a safe place to be. It was a time when young revellers saw their pay packets disappear within hours and, in some cases, saw fit to vent their subsequent frustrations on anyone who appeared in their paths. The most obvious targets were, of course, rough sleepers, who were often on the receiving end of kickings that led to spells in hospital.

On this occasion, though, the grapevine was unusually animated. Rumours were rife that changes at the top were afoot. This particular grapevine, the grapevine of the underclass… a section of humanity that went largely unnoticed elsewhere… was concerned with who ruled the roost in the local underworld.

The Lion Yard car park group gradually left their haven and filtered into the Market Square, where they could exchange news and views with *Big Issue* sellers, other homeless people and a few of the market traders.

The sort of news they exchanged tended to bypass the office workers, who either chose to stay at home most evenings or, if they went out, did so in close-knit groups. The 'freshers' tended to feel the effects of seeking too much refreshment the night before, and they, too, formed their own groups. Many of the university dons lived in their own erudite, esoteric and, in some cases, seemingly autistic worlds and ensured that Cambridge always had more than its quota of eccentrics. One of the quirkier dons had a penchant for approaching motorcycles that rested on walls or rails and moving the machines so that he could pass between the bike and its resting place.

The market traders had just finished setting up their stalls, which displayed merchandise that ranged from beads and bangles to bananas and Brussels sprouts. Some were sipping steaming hot mugs of soup, tea or coffee before business got under way in earnest.

One of the traders, who sold what passed for antique

177

jewellery and strained his vocal chords in an effort to emulate an Old Etonian, viewed the rough sleepers with disdain.

Another, a portly ex-boxer with cauliflower ears who spoke through a bent nose, went out of his way to offer the first to appear in the morning; a massive mug with PG Tips floating in boiling water.

Many of the traders shared, or contributed to, the underclass grapevine.

Frank was among the first to be seen at the stalls that morning. He had been unable to sleep and, knowing that Laura had family problems she wished to discuss with Peter, decided to make himself scarce.

Most of the traders knew Frank by now, or at least knew of him. They greeted him as one of their own, a compliment rarely paid to an outsider.

"I hear Billy Newton's on his way back," the ex-boxer said to him.

The news cheered Frank, who had taken a shine to the loquacious *Big Issue* seller. "That's great! I look forward to seeing him again."

The ex-boxer grinned: "You know it's all down to you, don't you?"

Before he could reply, a rough sleeper, who had sidled up to him, confirmed that this was the case. "Rumour has it that he put Einstein – that's Morris's right-hand man – out of action," he said. "Einstein was all set to give Billy a beating for talking to you and, well, it didn't work out that way!"

"Like I said, it's down to you!" the ex-boxer added.

"And you sorted out two other members of the X Factor, didn't you?" another market trader cut in.

Within a minute, a circle of ten and then a dozen, consisting of traders and homeless, had formed. Among the group was the wizened old woman with the cello whose ears seemed permanently glued to the ground.

A fair-haired woman left her fruit stall and offered her tuppenny worth: "I reckon the X Factor is losing its power. At the rate things are going, that bastard Morris will be on his own!"

The last observation led to startled looks, as it was known that harsh words spoken in the wrong place tended to reach Morris's ears and lead to 'punishments'.

"I've heard that a gang of Albanian sex traffickers are poised to take over," one of the rough sleepers said.

"The London 'Yardies' have shown an interest in Cambridge, too," another one added.

"So have the Triads," said another.

Frank then cut in. "Does anyone know where Morris is at the moment?" he asked.

"He's holed up in Wisbech."

"He's staying in a house that belongs to Tony Radford."

"Now there's another bastard! What can we do about him?"

The comments and questions came quick and fast.

"Someone told me you thumped Radford," said someone else.

Frank nodded. "Anyone know what he's up to now, or where he is?" he asked.

"You know where he oughta be, don't you?" a newcomer to the group volunteered. She was the shapely middle-aged woman who had attended Radford's sleazy party, at which she had been obliged to pay her rent 'in kind' and where a young leggy woman, Ellie, had received a savage beating from Tommy Morris.

"In jail, I suspect," said Frank.

"You're dead right! It should be jail, or worse."

There was more than a hint of a glint in Frank's blue eyes when he said: "Why don't you tell me what you know, and we'll see what can be arranged!"

The woman gave an account of what happened at the party, and added that Radford had charged exorbitant rents, failed to carry out repairs, intimidated tenants into quitting their homes and frequently used Morris as an 'enforcer'. In return, Morris was able to use Radford's properties as venues for drug deals, 'punishment parties' and other dodgy transactions.

"The bastard's just evicted me without warning. I've nowhere to go. I hope he rots in hell!" she wailed.

Another member of the group told how his ninety year-old mother had come home from a weekend away to find her bath, shower and WC had been removed and several front windows broken.

Another said he had been cheated at poker and forced to hand over his houseboat. Yet another told how Radford took over a bedroom one evening and forced himself on a young wife who could not repay her debts.

"Did anyone know my son Terry?" Frank asked, after a pause.

"Not really," the ex-boxer said, at length. "I think he came to my stall once or twice, but the only thing I know about him is that he worked for Hawkins for a while."

Frank pressed for details, but none were forthcoming.

"We wish we could help with that," a rough sleeper said. "In case you didn't know, we're all on your side!"

"Is there anything else we can help with?" a trader asked.

Frank paused for a moment before asking if anyone knew anything about Wainwright. The question was met with a multiple murmur. Everyone had heard of him, it seemed.

"He's a good copper who's gone to the bad!"

"He's on the take!"

"He's a mate of Radford."

"Whenever I see him, he seems to be pissed."

The trader who tried to sound like an old Etonian and had just decided to join the group said he had seen Wainwright and Radford exchange harsh words in a pub. "You were there at the time, weren't you?" he said to Frank.

"I certainly was, and the rumour that I thumped Radford shortly afterwards is true."

A loud cheer ensued. "Good on yer, mate!" the ex-boxer exclaimed in a tone of admiration that spoke for one and all.

"Pity you didn't thump Wainwright as well!" the fair-haired fruiterer observed.

"Trouble is he's always so pissed he wouldn't know anything about it!" a rough sleeper quipped.

Frank grinned: "I'd like to see him get his just desserts, all the same. I might not have thumped him yet, but there's still time!"

Everyone cheered except the wizened old woman with the cello. When the cheering stopped, all eyes were on her with an air of anticipation.

"I saw Wainwright knocking on the door of Hawkins last night. It was well after seven, and everyone who worked there had gone home." Everyone in the group listened open-mouthed.

The old woman continued: "About two hours later, he staggered out through the same door, obviously paralytic drunk, and I saw Hawkins usher him into a posh car and drive off with him."

CHAPTER 21

A big fist slammed into a Wisbech wall as soon as Tommy Morris hung up. Tony Radford had just updated him on what had been going on in Cambridge, and none of it was good.

He had already heard how Bob Wainwright's body had been fished out of the Cam. The news reached him at much the same time as it reached the whole of Britain. Bob Wainwright, to many a folk hero, had fallen from grace and into a watery grave after staggering drunkenly along a towpath. The media was full of it.

Morris mused for a while over whether there was more to the story than met the eye, though he was well aware of Wainwright's weakness for the bottle and, although it was hardly good news to him, the policeman's demise was no great surprise.

Of much more concern were the threats to his supremacy in Cambridge. When Radford expressed a desire to lie low in his 'Wisbech gaff' for a while, Morris said: "Fine. I have business to attend to in Cambridge."

On putting the receiver down, the familiar red mist descended. He shook, swore and lashed out. The only target in sight was a wall in Radford's property, which was left with a huge dent. Morris's knuckles, meanwhile, remained intact.

The main target Morris had in mind was the man who had invaded his manor and crossed his path once too often.

The object of his anger was back in Newmarket, in a bid to seek out Ernie Fosberg, the diminutive stable hand who seemed too terrified to talk. Laura was on her way to Cheltenham to look up an ailing aunt and offer respite for her sister, who was now effectively a full-time carer.

Frank and Peter had been busying themselves trying to learn more about Dominic Hawkins. What little they could find on record confirmed that he was in his mid-fifties and revealed that he had been born and bred in Cornwall, was privately educated and had never married. His academic record was outstanding, as was his sporting prowess and prominence in the school's cadet force. Particularly notable was his ability as a marksman with a rifle and his knowledge of weaponry in general.

No information was forthcoming about his parents, however, and another mystery was the fact that Hawkins left school during the middle of the middle term while he was a sixth-former and went to live in Colombia.

About fifteen years later, he returned to Britain but chose to live in East Anglia rather than the West Country. His Latin American business ventures, whatever they were, had made him immensely wealthy and, armed with a PhD in estate agency and property management, it was not long before he became the region's major player in this field.

"I think you could say there are gaps to be filled!" Frank observed with a wry smile.

"There certainly are," Peter agreed. "Perhaps it's my turn to pay our pillar of the community a visit."

"You'll probably get a load of flannel, and that's assuming you get to see him," Frank said ruefully. "Best of luck, anyway!"

Peter's smile was similar: "We'll see, but at least it's worth a try!"

Frank decided his best bet was to head straight for the Horse and Jockey Café, in the high street, where he and Laura had managed to find Fosberg on their previous visit to Newmarket, rather than the John Smith Stables, with its unhelpful guard and forbidding fences and gates.

He was in luck. His quarry was on a stool, gazing disconsolately through a window. On seeing Frank, he looked both surprised and surprisingly pleased.

Frank was quick to grasp the nettle. "Are you going to talk to me this time, or are you going to make another run for it?"

Ernie Fosberg's face turned purple. "I'm not going anywhere!" The words were forced out through a high-pitched lisp and a stutter, and Frank could see he was consumed with resentment and rage.

"I can see you're not a happy bunny!" said Frank. "What's up? Trouble at the stables?"

"You could say that."

"Why, what's happened?"

"I'm finished there. I wouldn't go back there if they offered to double my wages."

"Who did the finishing?"

The last question led to tears welling up in Ernie's eyes. "They did. They didn't actually sack me, as such, but they made it clear they didn't want me around no more, and made it impossible for me to stay."

"Who's 'they' and what did they do?"

Ernie hesitated for a moment. "That's a good question. At first, I thought it was the head groom. The security bloke at the gates, the tall bloke who dresses like a commissionaire… you might have seen 'im… slapped me around after word got out that I'd been talking to you, and when I complained to the head groom 'e just said it had been on instructions. After that, 'e went out of 'is way to make my life a misery."

"What did he do?"

"Everything he could think of. He gave me every crap job under the sun and criticised everything I did every day. He even mucked up my holiday plans – saying that if I didn't like it, I knew what I could do."

Frank looked searchingly into Ernie's eyes and could see he was genuinely upset. He had already guessed that the bullying head groom had been acting under instructions.

"After several days of this, I asked to see Mr Hawkins and told him about the problem," Ernie continued. "I don't know him that well, but he had always struck me as being a gentleman and I thought he would be sympathetic."

The tears returned, and Frank urged him to continue.

Ernie went pale. "He wasn't sympathetic at all, just the opposite. He got really nasty, even vicious. I'd never thought for a minute that Mr Hawkins could be anything but gentlemanly!"

"What did he say?"

"He swore at me, threatened me with violence, told me I was a liability and suggested that it might be best if I packed my bags and cleared off."

"What happened then?"

"After that, Mr Hawkins went out of his way to pick on me, and make my life a misery, and, after a couple of days, I could stand it no more and walked out."

Frank rubbed his chin speculatively. "Can you think of any reason why Mr Hawkins' behaviour changed so suddenly?" he asked.

"Yes, I think there is a reason. There'd been a rumour round the stables that Mr Hawkins was having problems of some sort, and, as a result, he had started to get jumpy."

"Any idea what those problems were?"

The two men eyed each other for what seemed an eternity. Frank could sense there was something else that Ernie wanted to get off his chest, but was not sure whether he dared to. "Go on! Go for it!" he eventually urged. "We're on the same side!"

Ernie allowed himself a sharp intake of breath and gave a massive sigh. "There is something else, but I'm not sure about it. I might have got it all wrong."

"Don't worry about that, I'm all ears!"

"OK, here it is. I've heard talk about the guvnor, that's Mr Hawkins, having trouble with 'is business in Cambridge. I've only heard bits and pieces of conversation involving the gaffer, the head groom, the security men and others at the stables that the gaffer Mr Hawkins can't rely on his contacts the way he used to. I've also heard whispers about drug deals, and I think I once overheard

Mr Hawkins talking on the phone about a shipment from Colombia."

"Do you have any names you can give me?"

"Yes, I know 'es had contact with that famous copper who was found drowned, Wainwright. I've also 'eard the names Radford and Morris mentioned."

Frank could feel his pulse racing. "Have you now? I've come across all three of these characters and have, for some time, suspected that Mr Hawkins has had dealings with them. I really appreciate what you've just told me."

Ernie smiled expansively. "The pleasure's all mine!"

"Is there anything you can tell me about my son, Terry?" Frank asked after a pause.

Ernie's smile was replaced by a pensive look. "You know Mr Hawkins is not married, don't you?"

Frank gave a start. "What the hell do you mean by that? You'd better explain that and fast!"

Ernie, fearful of rising hackles, responded immediately: "I think Mr Hawkins fancied your Terry, but your son would have none of it!"

The steely flash in Frank's blue eyes began to soften. "Do go on please!" he said softly.

"Sorry if I startled you," Ernie said meekly. "There's not much else to tell, really. I'm pretty sure Mr Hawkins had a hand in getting your son on drugs, and I think I saw him making an amorous advance once. But Terry wasn't interested. He didn't want to know."

Peter was not so lucky. Three telephone calls and three visits to the Hawkins office proved fruitless. "I'm afraid he's out of the office, I can't tell you where he is and don't know when he will be back," he was told each time.

He desperately wanted to help for all sorts of reasons. First and foremost was a compellingly urgent desire to cement his relationship with and prove beyond doubt his love for Laura.

Laura had come into his life while in a bad place, and was still feeling the effects of her parting from Frank. Laura and Peter first met purely by chance on a train, and the rapport they struck up was virtually instant. He happened to hit it off with Terry, too, and Peter was now deeply regretting his failure to understand how troubled the teenager had been. Perhaps he could have helped him through his drug addiction and done more to assume the role of the father he so sorely missed. Perhaps Terry would then still be alive?

Paradoxically, Peter had, to all intents and purposes, been married to the armed forces. There had been failed relationships in the past, not to mention the odd fling, but none were allowed to interfere with his career until Laura entered his life. Now his marriage to her was everything.

There was no doubt in his mind that when Frank came back on to the scene, Laura still had feelings for him. Peter was worldly enough to appreciate that such feelings were inevitable, and realised that even if Frank did pose some sort of threat, a hostile attitude towards his potential rival would probably be counter-productive.

In any event, Peter felt a sense of affinity towards Frank and even liked him. Both had military backgrounds and both had been temporarily married to their careers. Peter had never suffered from PTSD admittedly, but he had witnessed what the effects could be and heard many a tale of how the horrors of war could take their toll.

He wished he could help lead Frank out of his personal hell, and he knew Laura wished this, too. He knew Laura felt an unjustified guilt at times of being unable to help, and he wanted to lead Laura away from that guilt and make the most of the latest chapter in her life.

Peter was himself consumed with an urge to establish himself, in Laura's eyes, as 'Peter the rock'. His own life had been a lonely one. His parents, both personnel in the armed forces, had never stayed in one place for more than a year. They had died shortly after his recruitment into the RAF, and Peter's unsettled, almost nomadic, existence continued as he rose through the ranks and eventually became a captain.

Now in his fifties, Peter was living a settled existence for the first time. He had left the RAF four years ago, found a job as a representative for an insurance company and had lived in the same house in Cambridge for three years.

The situation he found himself in now gave him a sense of excitement, even danger, he had not felt since leaving the forces.

He likened the task of finding out more about Hawkins to a military mission. The fact that Hawkins was away from the office was, in no way, going to deter him. Laura was in Cheltenham and Frank was in Newmarket, and there was to be no turning back. It was time for him to take the initiative.

Peter grabbed a seat near the window of a coffee bar that looked out on to the Hawkins office. He noticed that to one side there was an iron gate and a narrow path leading to a wall and two dustbins that leaned against it. All but one of the side windows was barred. The exception was a larger window above which could be reached via a small sill. It offered just enough room for a man to crawl through headfirst. Peter still had the agility to do this.

The wait in the coffee bar seemed interminable. Eventually, however, the stream of callers to the office petered out and the staff filtered through the front door from inside and left for home. Once the massive double-fronted entrance was slammed shut, Peter felt ready to make a move.

His military training served him well. Scaling the gate and climbing onto the windowsill were still well within his compass. Peter was able to use a small crack at the top to prise open the unbarred window and enter headfirst. An outstretched hand found a sill on the other side and he was able to land feet first and almost noiselessly onto the floor.

The light from a torch he had brought along told him he was in a corridor. An assortment of photographs, most of them relating to horseracing, hung on the walls. One of the doors led to the front reception area. Peter guessed that the kind of information he was seeking was more likely to be found elsewhere, and he used his torch to locate other doors. One was locked, another turned out to be the entrance to a cupboard and a third led to a small room with a table, two chairs, a carpet and nothing else.

The fourth was the entrance to Dominic Hawkins' opulent office, and, after using a pin to open the lock, Peter could easily see why Frank had been impressed with it.

After running the torch light round the room, Peter

made a beeline for the monolith of a desk and started to open drawers. The top of the desk had just been polished, and was clear apart from a telephone and a row of gavels. The drawers were locked, and Peter made use of his pin again.

The first drawer he tried contained a ledger, a diary and a selection of stationery. Entries in the diary included a reminder to contact Pedro Alvarez in Colombia. Another referred to a meeting with Tony, Tommy and Bob.

What was inside the second drawer made Peter give a start. At the top of a pile of papers was a photograph of Dominic Hawkins and Terry Pugsley standing either side of a regal black stallion. Terry, looking thin and gaunt, was looking expressionlessly ahead. Hawkins was gazing at Terry in a way that suggested far more interest in the young stable hand than in the camera or the horse.

Peter picked up the picture and, startled as he was, immediately dropped it. As he got on his hands and knees in an attempt to retrieve it, something heavy descended on his head and sent him into oblivion.

CHAPTER 22

A sense of outrage that went even further than the 'underclass grapevine' dominated the conversation in the Market Square, and elsewhere for that matter, the following morning.

Even the news of how Wainwright's body had been fished from the Cam took second place.

A group of drunken revellers had rounded off their night of what they passed for fun by urinating on a group of rough sleepers on Christ's Pieces and given them a kicking when one of them protested. Two of the rough sleepers had to be rushed to Addenbrooke's Hospital with serious head injuries, and their lives were in the balance.

"Who would do such a thing?" a well-heeled office worker asked while standing near the stall manned by the ex-boxer.

The latter shook his head gravely. "There was a gang of six or seven who did it, I believe," he said.

"Two of them were only about fourteen or fifteen, by all accounts," the fair-haired fruiterer added.

"All pissed out of their minds, I suppose!" said Frank.

"I hope they get caught," a rough sleeper who had

spent the night in the Lion Yard car park, said, "though I don't suppose they will."

"Not a chance!" the *Big Issue* seller Kirk commented vehemently. "They all legged it long before the police knew anything about it."

The word 'police' caused the conversation to switch for a moment to the subject of how Bob Wainwright met a watery grave.

Frank, who had returned from Newmarket to an empty house, or, to be precise, garden, in Richmond Road, and was keen to locate Peter and exchange notes, said he knew Hawkins and Wainwright had jointly organised the latest Cambridge Crimewatch, and asked if anyone knew of any further dealings they might have had.

"I don't think there were any," one of the scruffier rough sleepers said. "That Hawkins feller's a bit toffee-nosed, by all accounts, and he tends to look down on people, even working-class folk heroes like Wainwright. He certainly turns 'is nose up at Radford, that's for sure!"

"I bet he does," said Frank. "Has anyone seen Radford lately?"

"No, but I've heard the fuzz want to talk to him," another *Big Issue* seller, who had just appeared, volunteered.

"Why's that?"

"Something to do with holding a sleazy party, at which a young girl was badly beaten up. I've heard a whisper that it was Tommy Morris who did it."

The very name caused Frank's muscles to tense up. "I haven't seen him for a while. Is he still around?"

"I've heard he's been away, but is on his way back," another rough sleeper told him.

"I've heard he wants to see you," another said "…and it won't be to talk about the weather!"

Frank's muscles tensed up again, though he remained poker-faced. "Bring it on!" he said. Then, in almost the same breath, he asked if anyone had seen Peter Andrews. He suspected that the name rang no bells with the circle of people he was standing with, but felt it was worthwhile asking all the same.

And, once more, it was the old woman with the cello who provided an answer. "Is he white-haired, fifty-ish and fit-looking?" she asked.

"Yes, that could well be him."

"I saw him yesterday evening, climbing over the gate at the side of the Hawkins office. God knows what he was up to!"

"That sounds like him all right," said Frank. "I'd like to know what he was up to myself!"

Silence reigned for what seemed longer than the thirty seconds it actually was. No one, not even the woman with the cello, could provide an answer.

"I know where he is, and he's keen to talk to you in private," a new voice from just behind Frank could be heard. It belonged to a gangly, pimply-faced young man whose face looked as if it had been ravaged by years of unhealthy living. His speech was slurred. Frank had never seen him before, and could sense he was being eyed with suspicion by everyone around.

"I'm all ears," Frank said to him.

"You can find Peter Andrews on Coldham's Common, behind a hedge that's near a pub," the pimply-faced young man said.

"Why would he want to meet me there?"

"He has something secret to say. He wants to be alone with you."

Frank looked him in the eye, before saying: "That doesn't stack up!"

The young man turned his face away and could only barely be heard to say, "That's the message I've been asked to give you," before slipping away and melting into a slowly growing crowd of shoppers.

A dozen pairs of eyes tried to see where he had gone, but without success.

"I wouldn't believe a word from that one," the ex-boxer, who was clearly voicing the view of everyone around, said. "He's a low life who'll do anything for a quick fix."

The woman with the cello, her face etched with concern, added just two words: "Be careful."

A throbbing head, sore limbs and an inability to move greeted Peter when he woke up. He had been tightly tied to a wooden chair, and the rope was cutting into his calves and upper arms. The room he was in was cold, damp and dimly lit, and there was the smell of earth all around.

"I think 'es starting to wake up, sir," a rough East Anglian voice could be heard to say.

The click of a switch followed, and Peter was half-dazzled by the light of a big bulb above him.

"Thank you, George. You can go now," an urbane, mellifluous voice replied.

The burly security man departed. Dominic Hawkins emerged from behind the chair to which Peter was tied, stood over the captive and gazed downwards for the best part of a minute.

Then, without warning, he delivered a backhand slap that had the chair and its occupant doing almost a full somersault. The slap was followed by a kick of awesome power to the stomach.

Hawkins watched Peter retch while trying to writhe, before, with one easy movement, restoring the chair to its upright position.

"You and your friend from the West Country have been an infernal nuisance," he snarled.

Peter was momentarily unable to reply.

"Lost for words, are we?" Hawkins sneered. "Never mind. I must confess, however, to being impressed with your agility. Gaining entry to my premises the way you did can have been no easy task, especially for a man of your years!"

"How very kind of you!" Peter now managed to retort, albeit painfully. Every syllable entailed effort.

"Yes, isn't it?" Hawkins said coolly, before his eyes narrowed. "Now tell me what the hell you are doing here?" he rasped.

Peter made a short study of his surroundings and saw stone walls and a concrete floor, and guessed he was in a small cellar. "Looking for the truth about your love life," he then said.

The retort led to another slap and several kicks. Hawkins rendered the chair upright once more before strolling towards a small table, on which were half a dozen gavels. He used one of them to light a cigar.

"I've been doing some research of my own," he said.

197

"You're ex-RAF and married to Laura, former wife of Frank PTSD Pugsley and mother of Terry, who worked for me for a while. Terry seemed a good lad at first, but he got a bit too nosy and then made matters worse by showing an interest in one of my stable girls."

"Poor you!" a defiant Peter said with heavy sarcasm. "That must have made you frightfully jealous!"

Hawkins raised his hand once more, but, after hesitating for a moment, walked to the table and picked up another gavel.

"It's amazing what you can do with these instruments." There was now a gloat in his tone. "There's no need to reserve them for auctions only. They can be customised to fulfil a multitude of roles. This one, for example, can be used to shoot poison darts."

"Very clever!" said Peter. "Perhaps you could tell me what the point is."

"An unfortunate turn of phrase, if I may say so, especially given these circumstances. Quite a number of my gavels have points to them, and they're all pretty lethal!" Hawkins picked up a gavel that propelled knives, another with a steel blade and two others that fired bullets, and demonstrated how each of them worked.

"I'm surprised you didn't use one of them on Terry!"

Hawkins laughed loud, long and maniacally. "Do you see this one?" he said, pointing to a gavel with a mother of pearl handle. "Do you?" It contains a needle that can be used to administer the most lethal cocktail of drugs imaginable. Just one jab can be fatal."

"You must be sick in the head!" said Peter.

"And you sound confident to the point of stupidity!"

Hawkins retorted. "Perhaps you think your friend Pugsley is about to come to your rescue. If you think that you are deluding yourself. I have got young Tommy taking care of him and you're never going to see him again. Not in this world, anyway!"

Frank was under no illusion about the likelihood of him walking into danger. He did not trust his informant, who had 'weasel' written all over him, and he knew full well that, in any case, Peter would not ask for a remote rendezvous when it was just as easy to meet in his Richmond Road garden. He knew that, sooner or later, there would be a confrontation ...almost certainly a full-on one... with Tommy Morris, and all the signs pointed to the fact that this was about to take place. The woman with the cello had warned him to be careful and, given the degree of danger, she was right to do so.

But this was a confrontation that Frank felt he could not avoid, even if he wanted to. Frank had come to Cambridge in search of truth and justice. There was little doubt that Morris could provide at least some of the answers, and Frank had made it his mission to beat those answers out of Morris.

The initial problem was that, although he had little doubt that it was Morris and not Peter who had expressed a desire to meet him, he did not know when and was not entirely sure where. The message delivered by the 'weasel' had been vague, to say the least.

After some deliberation Frank decided to cycle to Coldham's Lane, which overlooked the common, in a bid to locate Morris. On reaching that road, he pedalled uphill.

At the top, he was greeted by a young man with a skinhead haircut who told him he could find Peter in The Wrestlers in Newmarket Road. Once inside The Wrestlers, a barman handed him an envelope containing the message: "Meet me inside the Leper Chapel at 1pm." It was now 12.30, and Frank reckoned he could reach the chapel within a few minutes.

The pub was half-empty, though every eye inside seemed to follow Frank as he approached the bar, spoke to the barman, opened the envelope, read the note and then walked out. If Frank had read the note out loud, none of the punters would have been surprised by what it said, and the buzz of anticipation would have been just the same.

Frank reached the rendezvous a quarter of an hour early, giving him time to check the lie of the land. The chapel doors turned out to be locked, and there was no sign of life anywhere nearby. By now, he was convinced it was Morris he was about to meet and not Peter. Any smidgen of doubt was soon removed by the sound of an approaching motorcycle that came to a halt in the road above and the sight of Morris bounding down the steep stone steps.

The drugs dealer was greeted with the words: "Where's Peter Andrews?"

The response was a sneer. "Oh dear, oh dear, oh dear! You must be terribly disappointed to be seeing me instead!"

"I'm not disappointed at all," Frank said coolly. "On the contrary, I've been wanting to see you for some time."

"Good," said Morris, as he took off his leather jacket. "Your wish has been granted!"

Frank took off his jacket, too. "I still want to know where Peter is," he rasped. "Are you going to tell me, or am I going to have to kick it out of you?"

Tommy Morris stared speculatively at his outspoken adversary, before replying with a chuckle: "Peter Andrews is busy meeting his maker and you're about to do the same!"

The two men eyed each other before Morris threw a punch and aimed a kick. The punch and kick were both parried, as were Frank's counters. Morris then kicked one of Frank's shins. The kick caused a sharp pain, and Frank was well aware that more kicks in that area would eventually deaden his legs and bring down his defences elsewhere. So retaliation in kind was the only answer.

More kicks and punches followed, along with jabs with thumbs and fingers and blows with the edges of hands. Many of the kicks and blows missed, but some landed and caused damage that would be felt for days afterwards. But there was no sign of anyone gaining ascendancy.

After about a quarter of an hour, Tommy Morris took a sudden backward step and said: "Hang on a minute! You've put up quite a fight, and I might just let you off!"

"Why the hell would you want to do that?" Frank's anger had in no way dissipated, though he could not fail to notice the grudging respect being accorded to him.

"You've no doubt heard that I head up the X Factor in Cambridge, which happens to have a vacancy or two just now," Morris said. "I might be prepared to offer you a position in the organisation. After a trial period, I might even make you my deputy."

Frank's reply was far from receptive. "If you think your

offer's flattering, you couldn't be more wrong. All it does is show that you think I have a screw loose like you! So go to hell!"

Morris nodded slowly, and then, moving like a coiled spring, aimed a flying kick which Frank barely avoided.

As Frank prepared to launch an attack of his own, a blow to the back of the head brought him to his knees. The last words he heard before losing consciousness were, "I told you to keep out of it!"

CHAPTER 23

"I reckon Morris was all in when you got knocked on the head," said Billy Newton.

"He had precious little fight in him when we grabbed him and took him to the nick," agreed Adrian.

"It was that whack on the head with my brolly that did the trick," Germaine proudly pointed out.

"Yeah, that seemed to knock the stuffing out of him," Billy conceded. "Good thing we turned up when we did, though."

"It sure was!" said Frank. "To say it was good to see you must be the under-statement of the century!"

"It's good to be back," said Brian Simmonds, the friend of Terry who had felt obliged to flee to Leicester.

The group were sitting in the back garden of Brian's mother's home in Benson Street. Frank's friends had moved the tent to that garden so they could keep an eye on the man who had to live outside. Laura and Peter's home remained unoccupied, with Laura away and Peter's whereabouts unknown.

Billy, Adrian, Germaine and Brian had all known that the Morris menace was waning, and, apart from being less fearful than hitherto, they all wanted to give what support they could to Frank.

The 'underclass grapevine' had been so reliable that they had heard how Frank was being lured into meeting Morris at the Leper Chapel. And they had been able to rescue Frank in the nick of time.

The loquacious Billy was keen to speculate that Morris was on the verge of losing his battle with Frank before the drug dealer's henchman intervened. The others agreed.

"He was as quiet as a lamb when we took him and his sidekick to the nick," he said. "It's about time he got his comeuppance!"

"A good whack on the head with my brolly might have had something to do with it!" a grinning Germaine suggested again.

"It undoubtedly did," Adrian said as he patted her fondly on a shoulder.

"Good for you!" Frank said. "I gather Morris is still at the nick, helping the police with a variety of inquiries."

"You're dead right there!" said Billy. "A lot of people who were too afraid to talk to the police for fear of retribution are now coming forward. A lot of rough sleepers and others are giving the fuzz information about threats, intimidation and beatings, and there's a young girl who Morris beat half to death at a party who is now prepared to tell all."

"I understand Tony Radford's being pulled in too," said Adrian.

"That's right," said Billy. "Radford was the one who had the party where the beating of the young girl took place, and he's also been pulled for suspected dirty deals or turning a blind eye to them. His secretary is being questioned, too."

At this point, all eyes were on Frank. The outsider from Bristol, who lived in a tent because he could not cope with being indoors for any length of time, was rapidly becoming the toast of the under-privileged. He had virtually dismantled the X Factor single-handed and played a major part in putting the skids under the hated Tony Radford and a 'top cop' who had gone to the bad.

Frank made it plain that there was still unfinished business to attend to. "What about Dominic Hawkins, our 'pillar of the community'? He's managed to keep his nose clean up to now, but it's becoming increasingly clear that he's involved in what's been going wrong and he might even be the force behind it all. And where's Peter Andrews? He was last seen climbing through a window of Hawkins' office, but has since disappeared off the face of the earth!"

Now it was Brian's turn to speak. "I've got one or two things I can tell you about Hawkins," the usually quiet young man said. "When I was in Leicester, I met someone who knew him at school in Cornwall."

"Did you now?" said Billy. "Something tells me that the enigmatic Dominic, the 'Mister Charisma of Cambridge', is about to be looked at in a new light!"

Everyone's eyes were now on Brian.

"The guy I met, Tony Phillips, is two years younger than Hawkins and, because two years is a lot of difference when you're at school, he did not know him well." Brian, who was himself considerably younger than those around him, chose his words carefully at first. But the excitement that lay below the surface soon bubbled over.

"He was head prefect for two years in succession, which is very, very unusual," he continued. "He was outstanding at class work and was so good at sport that he was captain of just about everything. He was also the school's top cadet and, apart from everything else, seemed to know everything about guns and all sorts of other weapons. The school was boys only, by the way."

"I should imagine all the other boys looked up to him," said Frank. "Was he popular?"

"He was certainly looked up to," said Brian. "But I'm not sure about popular because he was a bit of a mystery, too. Little was known about him, and some of the boys were afraid of him."

"I've heard a whisper that he suddenly fell from grace and had to leave in a hurry," said Frank.

"That's right!" Brian exclaimed excitedly. "There was a big scandal, and Hawkins suddenly disappeared halfway through a term."

"Why was that?" asked Frank.

"He got found out abusing some of the younger boys. It had been going on for a long time. The boys of his own age knew about it, but did not dare say anything, and one or two of them joined in."

"So how did he get found out?"

"Purely by chance!" Brian replied with a flourish. "The headmaster had to go out for some reason one evening, but he didn't tell his wife. The wife, who never usually went anywhere near the dormitories, happened to wander into Hawkins' private rooms ...that was a special privilege only for the head prefect... and found him having sex with a first-former."

"I should imagine that led to quite a few questions," said Adrian.

"It certainly did! The head's wife was horrified, there was a major inquiry and it soon became clear that Hawkins had been doing it on a big scale and for a long time."

"And getting away with it!" said Frank.

"That's right," said Brian. "The trouble was that Hawkins had huge power, and was able to get what he wanted through threats, bribery and blackmail. If a younger boy had got caught breaking a school rule, he might be made to do what he was told or face detention or perhaps be the subject of a note to a parent."

"That certainly explains why Hawkins left his school in a hurry," said Billy.

"I gather he then cleared off to Colombia," said Frank.

"That's what Tony Phillips said. No one at the school knew anything much about his parents, though it had been said they had contacts there. One rumour that was going about was that the Colombian contacts were shady in some way."

"What you say worries me," said Frank. "It's becoming increasingly apparent that Hawkins is an extremely dangerous man, and I'm worried that Peter Andrews has fallen into his clutches."

The group spent a moment digesting that thought.

"So what do we do now?" Adrian asked.

"The only thing we can do, as far as I can see, is confront him," Frank replied. "That might mean threatening him, putting the wind up him. Anyone know where he is just now?"

"Good question!" said Adrian. "He can be a pretty elusive character, it seems."

"Just a minute!" Billy suddenly exclaimed. "It's coming back to me! Hawkins is due to stage an auction at 3pm this afternoon."

The venue for the auction was the Hawkins home in Porson Road, where the last Cambridge Crimewatch had taken place. The gardens were there to be viewed again, but this time a large hall to one side of the house could be accessed and was the focal point of interest. Items on offer at the sale ranged from sophisticated farm machinery to silverware and jewellery. A subsequent auction of a row of old cottages was due to be held a couple of days later.

A variety of vehicles could be seen parked outside or near the gates by the time Frank and his friends arrived. Frank had expressed concern over the possibility of being indoors for an extended period, and the others had promised their support and urged him to attend.

As they were about to enter the premises, the news of a murder could be heard from a car radio. A man thought to be aged about fifty had been found in the River Great Ouse, near St Neots. He had been stabbed eighteen times with a long knife.

Frank had no doubt who the victim was. He was consumed with anger, and this, almost inevitably, set off the trigger that continued to blight his life. The voice urging him to 'Kill, kill!' invaded his head once more, and Frank put his hands to his ears. Fortunately for him, Adrian and Germaine knew him well enough to see the signs. They sat him down on a bench that faced the

Hawkins property's manicured front lawns and sat either side of him.

"Don't worry," Germaine said softly. "Let's just sit quietly for a while until you feel better." Frank took a dozen deep breaths and, much to everyone's relief, the feeling of tension subsided. Germaine agreed to stay with Frank for a little longer, while Adrian and Billy went off to attend the auction.

The quartet had all made a point of putting on clothes that suggested they were middle class rather than underclass, and Adrian and Billy were able to enter the auction room without becoming the subject of raised eyebrows.

Dominic Hawkins, with his much loved collection of gavels set out in a row in front of him, was at the helm as expected. Lot No.1, a small tractor, had just gone under the hammer.

Although as elegantly dressed in 'country squire mode' as ever, he looked haggard and seemed to have acquired ten years' worth of worry lines since his last appearance in public. The usual suave fluency that featured in the way he was known to conduct every sale was lacking, too. His speech was halting, even faltering, and, on one occasion, he closed a sale while failing to notice a late bid.

The sight of Frank Pugsley walking through the door caused Hawkins' face to be drained of all colour.

With a little help from Germaine, Frank had regained his composure. The rage remained, but it was now controlled and focused and Hawkins was in no doubt who was the subject of that focus.

And he could no longer deride reports that the redoubtable Tommy Morris had failed in his latest mission.

The suave auctioneer, renowned for his ability to remain composed in all circumstances, let his list of lots fall to the ground and shook so visibly that no one present could fail to notice. He looked towards a small door behind him, took a few steps towards it, turned round to gather up his gavels and fled.

Hawkins slammed the door shut on the other side and locked it just seconds before a bounding Frank reached it. The door led to a smaller room used for storage and with just one window. He clambered through the window at the very moment Frank knocked the door down, and ran in.

A chase ensued across lawns that resembled bowling greens, past picture postcard flower beds, fountains and rows of trees, and towards the cottage and stream that occupied the furthermost point of the property away from the main house.

Hawkins was still able to run with considerable athleticism, but there was to be no shaking off Frank and, on reaching the stream, the auctioneer turned and pointed the one gavel he had not dropped at the pursuer.

Frank could see that the gavel was the shape of a pistol. He instinctively ducked and brought his quarry down with a rugby tackle, leapt on him and knocked him half-senseless with a punch to the jaw.

The gun-shaped gavel fell into a dip in the grass beside the stream.

"You killed my son, Terry, didn't you?" Frank hissed. He could see his adversary had come round, and he was now standing over him. "Get on your knees."

Hawkins obeyed the instruction and Frank repeated his question. Failure to answer it led to a slap. "Talk, or I will kill you!" The interrogation had reached fever pitch.

Billy, followed by Adrian and Germaine, arrived at the scene just in time to witness something that no one could have expected.

The suave façade that had served Dominic Hawkins so well for decades, perhaps even a lifetime, collapsed and the man on his knees became a gibbering wreck.

"Don't hit me again! Please don't hit me again!" Hawkins pleaded as tears streamed down both cheeks. "I can't take any more!"

Even the war-hardened Frank was taken aback.

But not for long. "If you don't tell me what you did to my son I'll do more than hit you. You will wish you'd never been born. Now tell me what you did to Terry, while you're still in one piece, and tell me now!" Frank showed Hawkins a clenched fist.

"All right, all right, I'll tell you!" the sobbing Hawkins said. "I had to kill Terry, I had no choice!"

"What do you mean no choice?"

Hawkins wept uncontrollably and mumbled something, which Germaine said later sounded like, "I want my mummy!"

Billy joined in the interrogation. "Frank means what he says. Talk! Or, if Frank doesn't kill you, I will!" His homely and usually friendly face was contorted with hate.

Dominic Hawkins, so used to being known as Dominant Dominic, looked up at Frank in the way a naughty schoolboy who had cheated with his homework and realised the game was up would look at his headmaster.

211

"He found things out about me!" he wailed.

"Go on!" Frank urged.

"He overheard a phone conversation and found out that I was doing deals with a drugs baron in Colombia. He also found out that I was gay and that I had a past that I hoped had been put behind me. I just couldn't let people know about these things!"

Frank and his friends gazed downwards at their pathetic enemy with withering contempt.

"So what did you do to him? Did you pump him full of drugs with one of your gavels? Is that how my son Terry died?"

"Yes, yes, yes! I'm so sorry!" The normally healthy Hawkins complexion was bereft of colour. The four friends looked at each other, and Frank stepped back a couple of paces.

Hawkins used the unexpected pause as an opportunity to dive towards the gun-shaped gavel that lay beside the stream. Frank tried to stop him, but it was too late.

Hawkins held the handle and pointed the other end towards his tormentors. "Stand back!" he screamed.

The quartet obeyed the instruction, and watched as the former pillar of the community turned the implement round, put the barrel end of it into his mouth and fired.

CHAPTER 24

Bedlam reigned for the rest of the day at the Hawkins property in Porson Road. The pulling of the trigger that spelt death for the top Cambridge businessman almost inevitably led to another trigger, causing a PTSD attack for Frank. The result was mayhem and chaos.

The sight of Hawkins' blood-spattered body on the path near the stream led to a succession of gasps and screams as the visitors to the auction realised something was amiss, went outside and eventually discovered what had occurred. A little later, sirens from police cars were stridently confirming that a drama of epic proportions was unfolding.

Once again, it was Germaine who managed to minimise the effects of the PTSD attack by gently guiding Frank away from the death scene and towards the van that she and Adrian lived in. Adrian stayed where he was to field questions from the police, and Billy was more than willing to be forthcoming as well.

News of the Porson Road drama spread throughout Cambridge and beyond at an alarming rate, with many living outside the city, famed for its halls of learning, viewing it in a different light.

The buzz of excitement was especially strong inside Cambridge Police Station.

Tommy Morris, already facing a catalogue of potential charges, was told what had happened to Hawkins and did his best to remain tight-lipped and emotionless. Evidence that he had been behind a high proportion of years of misdeeds in Cambridge began to mount, however. It soon became clear that Morris had been helping Hawkins sell shipments of heroin and cocaine from Colombia to people in the city.

Among the police finds was the gavel that doubled up as a dagger. The dagger had blood on it, and the blood group tallied with Peter's.

Members, past and present, of the once feared X Factor were brought in for questioning, as was Tony Radford and his secretary Maisie. Radford quickly realised that a lengthy prison sentence was on the cards, and decided his best policy was to admit to most of his misdeeds and to his dubious association with Bob Wainwright. He hoped he would be seen as a minor player, who was more or less forced to commit the crimes that he did!

Morris, on the other hand, remained defiant to the last, though the main question about his fate was not one of establishing guilt but of whether he should be committed to a mental institution.

Meanwhile, jubilation that Cambridge's most notorious drugs dealer had been apprehended was tempered by rumours that dealers from London were already showing renewed interest now that Morris was out of the way.

The new police chief, Crawford Mackenzie announced the setting up of a squad whose job it was to tackle any potential threats from drug dealers and others who felt they could fill the gap left by Morris. A new man from the 'Met' was appointed to head the squad, and, in a surprise move, WPC Steph Shawcross was invited to return from Billericay to join it.

Another move entailed strengthening links with the homelessness charities, Wintercomfort, Emmaus and Jimmy's Night Shelter.

Billy Newton, hailed as a local hero second only to Frank Pugsley was now a member of staff at Wintercomfort. One of his roles was to cement relations with the local police. Regular contact with WPC Shawcross, in particular, was envisaged.

Billy, along with Adrian and Germaine, had been accorded official accolades for their part in bringing Hawkins, Morris, Radford and their associates to book.

Brian Simmonds, meanwhile, was volunteering at both Wintercomfort and Jimmy's while seeking a university place to study criminology.

Brian and his mother were more than happy for Frank to continue to sleep in their garden, for the time being at least.

However, the latest PTSD attack had been a severe one, and Adrian and Germaine made the decision to pack his tent, bike and other possessions into their van and leave town. The decision was partly because they were nomadic by nature. The overriding reason, though, was their awareness that tranquillity for their friend was paramount just now. Journalists, both national and local, and representing all forms of media, were hunting for morsels of newsworthy information like jackals. Their most sought after source for 'copy' was, of course, the man who lived in a tent.

"The police and press can wait," Adrian declared as he motioned Frank to sit in the front passenger seat of the van, with Germaine occupying a seat at the back.

"Where are we going?" Frank asked with an air of not caring.

"No idea!" Adrian replied nonchalantly.

"Anywhere but Cambridge!" said Germaine.

The trio found themselves heading towards the Norfolk coast. Eventually they arrived at a remote spot near Overstrand, where they could park the van, pitch the tent nearby and chill out. Just before reaching that spot, Adrian had popped into a village store and ensured that they had enough provisions for the best part of a week.

On their way to Overstrand, Adrian had had to stop several times to allow Frank to 'go walkabout' and do battle with his demons.

On arrival, Frank rummaged through his hastily packed belongings, changed into a pair of shorts, a singlet, plimsolls and a tracksuit and went for a coastal run. Five miles later, he was back to be greeted with a steaming cup of tomato soup, a bread roll and two smiling faces.

For the next four mornings, Frank rose early from his sleeping bag and, after a series of deep breathing exercises and sometimes some star jumps and press-ups, took a run along the road or the cliff tops. At other times, there were picnics, meals cooked by bonfire, country walks and wildlife watching to be enjoyed.

Germaine made sure that a small portable radio she and Adrian had bought at a jumble sale some months ago kept everyone up to date with the news. The reception was appalling, but it was possible between electric stutters to hear news bulletins and interviews in Cambridge.

Billy Newton was more than willing to talk to the media, and some of his outspoken observations had to be edited in case they were libellous. A number of market traders, rough sleepers and *Big Issue* sellers were interviewed, too. Reactions of surprise and relief abounded, and praise was heaped upon Frank from almost every quarter.

One person who declined to be interviewed was Laura, now back in Cambridge. On hearing what had happened to Peter, she had hurried back as soon as she could and spoken to police. Frank shuddered to think how she had reacted when performing the tasking of identifying her husband's mutilated body, and part of him wished he could have been there to comfort her.

On the fifth morning of their Norfolk sojourn, Adrian echoed the thoughts of all by casually saying: "Time to move on, I guess."

Germaine agreed, but asked where to?

"We all need to go back to talk to the police, but the sixty-four dollar question is where do we go after that?" said Frank.

"I don't know about you, but I'm leaning towards Bristol," Adrian said.

"I'll go along with that," Germaine agreed.

Frank gave a cursory nod, and everyone instantly knew where his next port of call had to be.

Frank had never felt so nervous, uncertain or hesitant since the day he first saw Laura appear at that barracks dance at Aldershot all those years ago.

Adrian had parked the van a discreet eighty yards away from Laura's home in Richmond Road, and Frank approached the house with the faltering steps of the gangling youth he once was.

He did not know what he was going to say to Laura or how she would react to the sight of him on her doorstep. The journey from Overstrand to Cambridge had been spent thinking about the right words to express condolences over the death of Peter, and he had been unable to find them.

His mouth felt dry as he pressed the doorbell.

The sound of an upstairs window opening and closing followed by that of hesitant footsteps on the stair carpet could be heard.

After the front door was opened, Laura began to motion Frank to enter and then, almost simultaneously, realised that such a motion was inappropriate in this case.

Frank, who had made a point of donning a blue blazer, grey trousers and a white shirt, could not fail to notice that Laura, even when wearing a long-sleeved blouse and loose-fitting jeans, was as slim and shapely as ever.

She had aged since their last meeting, however. Her greying hair had been cut short and, perhaps because of the absence of make-up, Frank could see there were a few more wrinkles. Her eyes were tired-looking and tinged with the sort of redness that suggested she had been crying for hours.

Laura took a long look at Frank, too, making the latter feel uncomfortable. Frank did not know what she was thinking, or what to say.

It was Laura who broke the silence. "I hear you've made quite a name for yourself," she said. The tone was neither effusive nor hostile.

"I'm really sorry about what happened to Peter," Frank blurted. "Is there anything I can do?"

More silence followed.

"Well, I hope we can stay in touch," said Frank. He was now sounding desperate.

Laura looked into Frank's eyes, before saying with an air of resignation: "I don't think so."

"But why not?"

"We're not good for each other, or, at least, you're not good for me!" The sadness in her tone contrasted sharply with Frank's air of urgency.

"Aren't you at least pleased that I uncovered the truth about Terry's death?"

"Yes, I am, but it came at a cost, didn't it?"

"But Peter's death wasn't my fault! I didn't know he was…"

"That's not the point," interrupted Laura.

"What's the point, then?"

Tears welled up in Laura's eyes. "You just don't get it, do you?" she said. "You cause destruction wherever you go, or you could say destruction follows you wherever you are! I'm not saying it was necessarily your fault, though, in a way, it is. You have a problem, and you need help. But you won't get it, will you? You're just too stubborn! You say you can sort it out by yourself, but you can't!"

219

"All right, all right, I'll change! I can change, just you see!"

Laura sighed. "Maybe you can, maybe you can't. But you can't do it by yourself. You've got to get specialist help. I can't have you around any more under these circumstances."

"All right, all right!" Frank screamed. "I'll get help!"

"I'll believe it when I see it. You've said you'd get help before and somehow you've never got round to it. I'm sorry, I can't take it any more. I don't want you in my life!"

"But…"

"Please go! Just go! Stay out of my life!"

Laura closed the door, and Frank turned to make his way back to the waiting van. Laura went back upstairs and watched him go.

About halfway between the house and van, Frank turned and screamed: "I will get help. I really will get help, and I will do everything I can to get it sorted out. I can change!"

"I'll believe it when I see it!" Laura shouted back.

Laura saw Frank dejectedly approach the van and get in. A tear rolled down a cheek as she looked away from the window and towards an old photograph on her bedroom mantelpiece. It showed a ten-year-old Laura standing with her parents beside an Aldershot parade ground.

"I'll believe it when I see it," she murmured while studying the photograph.